"What's this? Do you come with the house?"

Max's question left Ginny struggling for composure. "In a manner of speaking, I do," she said, "but not in the way that you obviously think."

"I'd have said you were the obvious one," he remarked. "I asked you to leave—yet here you are in my bedroom. Very flattering, but can you restrain your ardor until after I've had my dinner?"

"You insulting swine!" Uncaring of the need to placate him, Ginny lashed out, "You have the most monstrous ego I've ever run across! I find you totally resistible, Mr. Hendrick. As for being in your bedroom, it's duty that brings me here, not desire. I'm your housekeeper."

"That's what you think," Max said smoothly. It took Ginny a moment to understand what he meant....

Other titles by

SARA CRAVEN
IN HARLEQUIN PRESENTS

Other titles by

SARA CRAVEN
IN HARLEQUIN ROMANCES

SARA CRAVEN

shadow of desire

Harlequin Books

TORONTO • LONDON • LOS ANGELES • AMSTERDAM
SYDNEY • HAMBURG • PARIS • STOCKHOLM • ATHENS • TOKYO

Harlequin Presents edition published December 1980
ISBN 0-373-10398-0

Original hardcover edition published in 1980
by Mills & Boon Limited

CHAPTER ONE

GINNY CLAYTON packed the last carton of groceries carefully into the back of the elderly estate car and slammed the rear door shut, with a smiling word of thanks for Mr. Murgatroyd who had helped her carry the boxes out of the shop. The sometimes reluctant engine started at the second attempt and the car moved away slowly, bumping over the cobbles before easing on to the road and disappearing out of the market square.

Mr. Murgatroyd, dourly returning Ginny's exuberant farewell wave, heaved a sigh before returning to the shop. His wife, busily pricing a new consignment of tinned fruit, looked up, and encountering his brooding look gave a sympathetic nod.

"It just doesn't seem right—a young lass like that, with all that responsibility." Mr. Murgatroyd poked a cereal packet back into line on a shelf with quite unnecessary vigour.

"There's not many her age would take it on," Mrs. Murgatroyd observed temperately. "The old aunt would have been put in a home, and foster-parents found for that young limb of a brother. She could have had a life of her own then."

"Instead of dogsbodying for that Mrs. Lanyon," Mr. Murgatroyd said fiercely. "That's all she'll be, Ida. A dogsbody." He seemed to relish the word in a gloomy way.

The Murgatroyds were both silent for a few moments, considering Ginny's employer, Vivien Lanyon, the widow of the last of a long line of a once wealthy and powerful local family. The Lanyons had lost their power and most of their wealth

long before Geoffrey Lanyon had been killed skiing in the
Swiss Alps, and although no one in the locality was able to say
precisely why such a deterioration in the family fortunes had
come about, nevertheless everyone agreed that it was not
because the Lanyons had ever been guilty of overpaying their
staff, or treating their tenants too generously.

They were not nor ever had been a popular family, and
although the local people admired the way Vivien Lanyon
was hanging on at the Manor, and even making a go of her
riding stables, they still agreed that she was a real chip off
the old block and no mistake, more like a Lanyon born than
a stranger who happened to have married into the family—
and no one was under any illusion that this was intended as
a compliment to the lady.

"And that sister," Mr. Murgatroyd continued. "What's
she doing about it all, I'd like to know?"

"She's an actress," Mrs. Murgatroyd said, as if that explained everything. "I saw her on an advert on the telly last
night. For hair spray." She affixed the last price label with
an air of relief. "Anyway," she went on, "it's none of our
business, when all's said and done, and there's a load of
soft drinks wants bringing in."

Mr. Murgatroyd nodded, and set off for the rear of the
shop in search of the soft drinks, but his mind even then
was still not completely on his mission. He sighed again. "It
just doesn't seem right," he muttered.

Ginny, driving home along quiet lanes, would have been
surprised to learn that she was the object of anyone's sympathy. For the past few months she had been unable to believe her own good fortune.

Yet "dogsbody" would have had a familiar ring. It was
the very word that their family solicitor Mr. Robson had
used when he had told her about the job at Monk's Dower.

"You'll be little more than a glorified caretaker, Ginny,"
he'd said, shaking his head. "I don't know whether I'm
doing the right thing in telling you about the position—only
it does include accommodation, and I know this has been
proving a problem for you."

That, Ginny thought, was putting it mildly. The worry of trying to find a home for herself, plus an elderly lady, a small boy and a disreputable dog, had been keeping her awake at night, and deepening the shadows under her large hazel eyes.

It was incredible and frightening how life could change almost in the twinkling of an eye, so that the security she had always taken for granted was revealed as the fragile and tenuous thing it had always been in reality.

Security had been life in the tall Victorian house in the quiet country town where she had been born, with her parents and younger brother Tim, and with Aunt Mary, who had occupied the top floor of the house ever since her retirement from a career in teaching at a girls' boarding school in the south-west of England.

It had been a quiet comfortable existence, and Ginny had found her progression from school to a secretarial course a peaceful one. She had never shared her older sister Barbara's hankering for the bright lights, but then, as she would have been the first to admit, neither did she share Barbara's dazzling good looks.

No one had really been surprised when Barbara opted for drama school in London, nor that when her course was finished she had stepped straight into a small part in a long-running hit in the West End.

Mr. and Mrs. Clayton had been delighted for her, and if they were disappointed that their glamorous eldest child so rarely found the time to come home to see them, they never admitted it. They seemed prepared to accept that Barbara now inhabited a different world, and took pleasure in her success, and the paragraphs that she now merited in the local paper.

But there had never been any question of Ginny following in her sister's footsteps. Not that she had ever had ambitions in that direction, but if she had then a glance in her mirror would have quickly established a more realistic point of view. Her brown hair hung straight and as shining as rainwater to her shoulders, and though her eyes were large

and heavily fringed with dark lashes, they were not otherwise remarkable, and nor were her other features. But, as
she had often cheerfully remarked, one raving beauty in the
family was quite enough, and she accepted without rancour
the nickname "Mouse" which her relatives bestowed on
her.

She enjoyed her secretarial course. She was enjoying,
with reservations, her first job in an accountant's office.
Even within the limitations of her environment, her life
seemed to stretch away in front of her, full of possibilities as
yet unexplored.

And then, one night of black ice, everything changed for
ever. A coachload of football supporters veered across a
dual carriageway and crashed into the Mini bringing Mr.
and Mrs. Clayton home from the house of some friends.
Mrs. Clayton was killed instantly, but Ginny's father lingered for a few days in intensive care.

Ginny coped because she had to, undergoing the ordeals
of funerals and inquests. But there was a greater ordeal to
come, one that no one had suspected. Mr. Clayton's small
business had been heavily in debt, and he had borrowed
from finance companies, not always wisely, using insur-
ances and even his home as security. To her horror, Ginny
learned that when all the creditors were paid, there would
be hardly anything left in the way of money, and that they
would no longer have a home.

In a way she was glad that her mother would never know
just how flimsy the outward fabric of her life had been. Her
father had never brought his business worries home with
him, and for Mrs. Clayton life had always been comfortable, with no shortage of little treats and luxuries.

But there was no escaping the fact that she, Ginny, was
now responsible for finding accommodation for them all,
and for earning sufficient money to pay the rent and support them.

Nor could she avoid the unpleasant truth that Barbara
was not prepared to help in any way.

Her sister had made that more than clear during the

brief time she had spent at home to attend the funeral.

"I think you're completely mad," Barbara had declared, stubbing out her cigarette in the saucer of her coffee cup. The sisters were in the kitchen having a bedtime drink the night before Barbara was due to return to London. "No one expects you to take on the responsibility for them all—a girl of eighteen. It's ridiculous!"

"But if I don't, who will?" Ginny asked mildly enough. Her head ached miserably and she felt drained of emotion. The last thing she wanted was an argument.

"Well, I won't for one," Barbara said bluntly. "There's no room at the flat and I have my own life to lead—my career to think of, thank you very much. And so should you."

"I haven't really got a career, just a job that I don't much care about." Ginny carried the coffee cups over to the sink and began to rinse them under the tap. She looked round at the neat, bright kitchen with its tiles and new kitchen units which Mrs. Clayton had been so proud of, and a sharp little pain twisted inside her like the turn of a knife. "But it's been experience, and I can look for something that pays rather better now."

Barbara's lips twisted. "You'll need something that pays like a bomb for what you have in mind. For heaven's sake, Ginny, see sense. You're biting off altogether more than you can chew. No secretary's salary in this neck of the woods is going to pay the rent for the size of place you'd need—always supposing you found somewhere, and that won't be easy. Where landlords are concerned, children and dogs are an anathema, take my word for it."

Ginny turned off the hot tap with intense concentration. "Which do you suggest that I have put down—Tim or Muffin?" she enquired.

"Oh, don't be a fool," Barbara snapped. "But you've got to be realistic. Just because Dad fancied himself as an amateur philanthropist, it doesn't mean that you have to follow in his footsteps."

"You mean Aunt Mary." Ginny reached for the tea

towel. "Doesn't it matter to you that she's losing her home as well?"

Barbara shrugged. "Of course," she said without any conviction. "But she can't rely on you to provide her with another one. She must see that. After all, she has her pension, and there are plenty of places catering for elderly women in her position."

"Nursing homes, I suppose, and seedy private hotels." Ginny dried a cup and hung it from the appropriate hook. "Would you really condemn her to that, Barbie? She was Dad's favourite aunt."

"But not mine," Barbara said coolly. "I don't know how Mother put up with her all these years."

There was a difficult silence, then Barbara picked up the thread again.

"And as for Tim—well, has it occurred to you that the Social Services might take a hand?"

"Yes, it has," Ginny said coldly. "It's also occurred to Tim, and he's worried sick about it. Some of the children at school have been telling him that he'll be taken into care— you know what insensitive little beasts they can be."

Barbara reached for another cigarette. "Would it be such an unthinkable thing?"

"Barbie!" Ginny was aghast. "You can't be serious!"

"I'm trying to be realistic," Barbara said sourly. "Face facts, Ginny. How can someone of your age be mother and father to an eleven-year-old boy? It's just not on."

"It has to be," Ginny said. "I've given Tim my word that we won't be split up."

"If you don't find another job and somewhere to live, the choice may not be yours," Barbara had pointed out coolly and unanswerably.

It was a fact that was haunting Ginny now that the first shock and grief of losing her parents was beginning to wear off. In a way, she was glad that the harsh practicalities of life were beginning to assume such importance, and make such demands on her time and energy, because they stopped her indulging in bouts of useless emotionalism and self-pity.

The very fact that Tim and Aunt Mary depended on her so heavily had lent her a strength and purpose she had never been aware of, but it had not blinded her to the realities of the situation.

She had wondered at first whether Barbara would be able to help financially, if in no other way, but she had soon been disabused of that notion. Her sister was about to go into rehearsal in yet another light comedy which would be taken out on tour before its West End opening, and no one could prophesy what its fate would be in the uncertain world of show business. It might provide Barbara with a steady income for many months to come, or, as she pointed out with unshakeable logic, it might fold almost at once, leaving her to join the dole queue. Whatever happened, she was in no position to commit any of her income.

Ginny was not altogether surprised. She had always been aware that there was a single-minded, almost ruthless streak in Barbara which set her apart from the rest of the family. Certainly their father had never possessed it, Ginny thought with a sigh, otherwise his affairs might not have been in the bleak state they were at the time of the accident.

At the same time, she knew that Barbara's view of her situation was a realistic one, and this was brought home to her in the weeks which followed. There were other jobs, but none that paid the sort of salary on which she could support a ready-made family, and finding another home was quite a different matter.

None of the flats and small houses she saw were large enough to accommodate them all, and those that were she could not afford. And, as Barbara had prophesied, few prospective landlords were prepared to consider a tenant with a child in tow anyway, and after the first few rebuffs, Ginny did not even dare mention the existence of Muffin, the mongrel dog, past puppyhood it was true, but certainly not past such anti-social habits as burying bones under sofa cushions and scratching paint off doors to facilitate his exits and entrances.

She had been very near to despair and worn out with the

effort of concealing it from Tim and Aunt Mary when Mr. Robson had phoned to ask her to call and see him at his office. Ginny had supposed it was to do with some detail about the sale of the house, which was proceeding with almost frightening speed.

When he had mentioned the job at Monk's Dower, she had hardly been able to believe her ears, even though he had warned her candidly that it would be no sinecure.

Vivien Lanyon, it transpired, was the client of a friend of his in the neighbouring market town. Monk's Dower had been in the Lanyon family almost as long as they had occupied the Manor House. Local history said that the name recalled the bitter period following the Dissolution of the Monasteries, when the Lanyon of his day had allowed some monks expelled from a nearby abbey to build themselves a shelter on a corner of his land. Here, it was said, they had settled, cultivating their plot of ground, and looking after the sick of the nearby parishes as they had always done. Eventually they died, one by one, and the house they had built reverted to the Lanyons who had used it as a dower house ever since.

"I gather Mrs. Lanyon plans to let the house on a long lease." Mr. Robson stared down at the gold fountain pen he was holding. "It's a large, rambling place—it's been added to in all kinds of ways over the years, and her plan is to let it with—er—resident domestic help included, as it were. The servants' quarters have been converted, I understand, into quite a pleasant self-contained flat, but the wages she is offering are far from generous. So far she has experienced considerable difficulty in finding anyone suitable to take on the job because of the poor money. The attraction as far as you are concerned, Ginevra, would be the accommodation. I am not personally acquainted with Mrs. Lanyon, but I cannot say whether I could recommend her as an employer from what I have heard." He paused.

"What exactly would I have to do?" asked Ginny.

"Make sure the house is kept clean and aired, and ready for occupation as and when the tenant required. But I would guess that covers a multitude of other sins as well." Mr. Robson gave her a kindly but rather rueful smile. "Mrs. Lanyon has the reputation, frankly, of demanding her pound of flesh and more. You might well find that you were little better than a dogsbody for her."

"Does she object to dogs?" Ginny asked swiftly, not really taking in the implication of his words, because her heart was beating with sudden excitement. Compared with her present problems, coping with a difficult and perhaps demanding employer seemed a much easier option.

"I hardly think so. She keeps a number of them herself, I believe, and shows them too. You could represent your dog in the capacity of a guard dog, perhaps. I understand her tenant is likely to be away a good deal."

Ginny had a mental image of Muffin—he of the flopping ears and eagerly proffered paw.

"I'm sure he'd make a very good guard dog," she said mendaciously. "Mr. Robson, I could kiss you!"

He sighed. "Don't be too grateful, my dear, until you find out more about it, but if you're interested, I can arrange an interview."

It only took half an hour in Vivien Lanyon's formidable presence to warn Ginny that all Mr. Robson's forebodings were probably quite justified. She was tall, blonde and attractive in a hard way, and she made it clear at the outset that Ginny was far from being what she had in mind as a caretaker.

"You're far too young," had been her first, incredulous reaction and Ginny had had to bring all her persuasive powers to bear to ensure herself a fair hearing.

"I wanted a couple really." Mrs. Lanyon had flung herself down pettishly on one of the silk-covered sofas in her drawing room. "The man to do the outside work and look after the garden, of course, but people don't want to work these days, it seems, and quite frankly I'm getting desperate, so I suppose I could give you a trial." She looked Ginny up and down and sighed. "The hours will be long, I give you fair warning, and rather uncertain, but the reduced rent you'd be paying reflects this, I think. The house itself has been taken for a preliminary year by a Mr. Hendrick, and you'd be answerable to him rather than me. He's abroad a good deal, and you'd have to see to it that the house was always ready for him at all times—fuel stocks replenished, staple foods and milk ordered—that sort of thing. I'd expect you to keep the house clean and tidy too, but the heavy work is being done by Mrs. Petty from the village. As for the garden—"she hesitated, tapping a varnished nail against her teeth"—I suppose I'll have to let you have Simmons one day a week."

"Perhaps Mr. Hendrick will take an interest in the garden," Ginny ventured.

Mrs. Lanyon gave a short laugh. "I hardly think so. He isn't the type to bother about such mundane affairs, but he likes the house and that's all that matters." She gave Ginny a long, hard look. "It's very quiet out here. The village is very small, and it's a long way to the nearest town. What will you do with yourself—a girl of your age?"

Ginny was tempted to reply that she felt her time would be fully occupied with the programme Mrs. Lanyon had outlined, but she curbed her tongue.

"I have my family to look after," she returned with a dignity which sat oddly on her youthful shoulders. "I shan't be bored."

"I wasn't thinking of that." Vivien Lanyon took a cigarette from the box on the table in front of her and lit it. "You realise you'll be sharing a house with a single man. I wouldn't want you to get—ideas." Face and voice were equally unsmiling as she said it, and Ginny felt a swift surge of temper rising within her which again she had to control. Instinct told her that Vivien Lanyon would not countenance an employee who answered back, and she needed this job and what it promised.

"I can safely say that my only idea is to do the job well and provide a home from my brother and my aunt," she said quietly.

Vivien Lanyon shrugged slightly. "I'm pleased to hear it. At least with your responsibilities, you should be dependable. You won't be likely to flit away as soon as the novelty wears off. Very well then, Miss Clayton—Ginevra." She glanced down at the letter of introduction which Ginny had brought. "What an extraordinary name!"

"I believe it's a form of Guinevere," Ginny said rather bleakly. "My mother used to love all the Arthurian legends."

"Really?" Mrs. Lanyon looked and sounded blank. "How fascinating. Now, when do you think you could start? Mr. Hendrick's tenancy begins next week, although he won't be taking up occupation immediately."

"I'm working out my notice now," Ginny told her. "I could start on Monday, using the weekend to move in—if that was all right?"

"Quite satisfactory." Now that everything was settled, Vivien Lanyon's voice was almost indifferent. "Call in at the office as you go out and Kathy my head girl will show you round the house. You have transport, I presume?"

"Yes." Ginny thanked heaven inwardly for the driving lessons which had been her father's seventeenth birthday present to her. She had passed the test at her first attempt and had been used to driving both the Mini, which had been a write-off after the accident, and the rather battered estate car which her father had used for work, and which she was determined to hang on to at all costs.

The term "girl" was something of a misnomer when applied to Kathy, Ginny discovered, when she was confronted by a large middle-aged woman who regarded her with something akin to pity on her weatherbeaten face.

"How do you do." She extended a hand which could have encompassed both Ginny's slender ones. "My word, she saw you coming and no mistake! How's a slip of a girl like you going to see to a great barn of a place like that?"

Ginny bit her lip. "I'm not afraid of hard work."

"You don't need to be, working for her." Kathy got up from the desk where she was working with account books and ledgers. "I suppose you want to see round the place—see the worst, eh?" She took a bunch of keys from a board

by the door. "Mind you," she went on, leading the way
through the stable yard round to the front of the house
where Ginny had left the car, "it's a wonder to me that her
ladyship has taken you on at all—but I suppose she can't
afford to be choosy at the money she's offering."

"Thank you." Ginny did not know whether to be amused
or insulted at the older woman's forthright remarks. "I assure you that I'm perfectly capable."

Kathy shrugged. "Makes no matter to me, dearie,
whether you are or not. As for her, you could be Mrs.
Beeton the second, and she still wouldn't take you on. She
likes her female staff to be battered old warhorses like me,
not clear-skinned young girls—especially when there's a
man around."

Ginny was startled. "You mean Mr. Hendrick?"

Kathy gave an exaggerated sigh as she settled herself into
the passenger seat. "None other. He's all man, believe me.
Madam there couldn't wait for him to sign the lease."

"I see," Ginny said slowly, as she started the engine.

"Well, I hope you do, ducky. No use in looking for
trouble, is there? And she marked him down as hers the
moment she laid eyes on him."

Kathy might be appallingly indiscreet, but she seemed
friendly enough, and Ginny laughed.

"I'm not setting up in competition against her, believe
me."

"You couldn't, dearie." Kathy's tone was dry. "You'd be
left at the start. If she'd thought there was the slightest
danger you'd be looking for another job."

As they drove down the narrow lane leading to Monk's
Dower, it occurred to Ginny that this was the first time her
brown mouse looks had ever actually stood her in good
stead, but this was not a particular comfort to her. A small
flicker of rebellion stirred inside her at being so easily dismissed, but she stilled it. Her attractions, or lack of them,
were the last thing that should be on her mind at this point
in time.

Monk's Dower was large and rambling, built on three

sides of a courtyard in a variety of styles reflecting the periods when additions had been made. Her heart sank a little as she followed Kathy from room to room, because it was neither labour-saving nor convenient. There were open fires in the principal rooms, and wide expanses of ancient polished floorboards. Most of the furniture seemed old-fashioned without being antique, but there was a mellow air about the place which not even the slightly dank smell of disuse could dispel.

The kitchen was slightly more hopeful. It has been modernised and furnished with attractive pine units, and there was a modern wood-burning kitchen range as a centrepiece. The roomy walk-in pantry contained a large deep-freeze, Ginny noticed, and she supposed she would be expected to supply this with the kind of food a bachelor would need—whatever that was. Convenience food, she surmised vaguely, and chops and steaks.

"The place smells damp." Kathy sniffed the air. "It wants living in—fires lighting. I told you it was a barn, didn't I?"

"Yes," Ginny acknowledged. "But it has character—and it could be lovely, if someone cared about it."

Kathy's lips twisted derisively. "The someone being you, I take it? Well, let me give you some good advice, ducky. Don't knock yourself out—and don't break your heart either. I've worked for her ladyship for years, but I've seen others come and go. Just do what you're asked and take your money, but don't make any special effort, because you won't be thanked for it."

Ginny tried to smile in reply, but Kathy's cynicism disturbed her. She wondered how many years she had worked for Mrs. Lanyon. Certainly she seemed to know her employer only too well.

She drove home feeling rather depressed when she should have been on top of the world, but when she arrived back at the house she was thankful that she had taken the job, because a social worker was waiting for her, being entertained rather stiffly by Aunt Mary who had been brought up to believe that Heaven helped those who helped themselves, and who disapproved of the Welfare State on principle.

The interview which followed was a rigorous one, because the children's officer clearly did not believe that Ginny was old enough or responsible enough to be head of any sort of family. She listened with frank scepticism as Ginny outlined her plans and gave details of the new job.

"You surely don't expect to maintain yourself and a growing boy on a wage like that!" was her immediate reaction.

"Certainly not," said Ginny, who hadn't even got around to considering the nuts and bolts of the situation. She cast round wildly in her mind for inspiration. "I—I'm going to be left with a lot of time on my hands, so I thought I'd—start a typing agency," she finished on a sudden gulp of relief, which she hoped had not been noticed by her inquisitor.

"I see." The social worker looked frankly nonplussed, and after a few more rather desultory questions, took her leave, announcing brightly that she would "be in touch."

"I hope," Aunt Mary said reprovingly once they were alone, "that you haven't deceived that unfortunate woman, Ginevra. Have you actually made enquiries into the need for such an agency?"

"Well, no," Ginny said rather guiltily. "But I'm sure there are lots of people around who haven't enough work for a full-time secretary. I shall advertise."

"Hm." Aunt Mary pursed her lips. "I hope your advertising is successful, my dear child. Our visitor's remarks had a certain justice, you know. Tim is growing fast, and approaching the most expensive period in his life. It seems to me this post you've obtained is going to entail a great deal of work for very little return. Are you sure you've made the right decision?"

"Part of the return is a roof over our heads," Ginny said gently. "That's the most important thing."

"A roof, nevertheless, that's dependent on the whim of others." Aunt Mary shook her head. "Not a comfortable situation, but we'll have to hope for the best." She hesitated for a moment, then reached down for the capacious black leather handbag which accompanied her everywhere. "I've taken the precaution of writing away to a few places. You're a good child, Ginevra, but I wouldn't wish to inflict a greater burden on you than you're able to bear."

"What do you mean?" Ginny glanced at the sheaf of papers her great-aunt was extending to her. "The Sunnyview Home for the Aged," she read aloud in tones of disgust. "Oh, Aunt Mary, how could you! Your home is with us—you know it is."

"My home was with your dear parents," Aunt Mary corrected her, her back a little straighter than usual. "You're very young, Ginevra, and you have every right to a life of your own." She paused. "I'm not by nature an eavesdropper, but I happened to come downstairs one night while your sister was here. I couldn't avoid overhearing what she was saying, she produces her voice extraordinarily well—part of her stage training, I suppose."

"Aunt Mary!" Ginny was aghast. "You—you really mustn't take any notice of Barbara. We see things from completely different angles and...."

"I'm aware of that," Aunt Mary said rather acidly. "If you shared her viewpoint, this conversation would probably not be taking place. But she was not entirely in the wrong, although I found her mode of expression rather hurtful. Are you quite sure that Tim is not more than sufficient responsibility for you?"

"Quite sure." Ginny's voice was firm. "Aunt Mary, you can't let me down. I—I need you. No matter what I told that woman, I'm going to have my work cut out looking after that house. If you could help with the cooking and—just be there when Tim gets in from school," she ended on a note of appeal.

"I shall be pleased to do whatever I can." Aunt Mary allowed her firm lips to relax into a smile. "And I'm not entirely decrepit, Ginevra. I daresay I could make beds and help with the dusting, as well."

Impulsively Ginny put her arms round her great-aunt and hugged her. Aunt Mary did not, as a rule, welcome random demonstrations of affection, but this time when Ginny released her, she looked pink and pleased, even though she said robustly, "Go along with you, child."

In the intervening two months, Ginny thought, things had worked out better than she had ever dared hope. The move to Monk's Dower had gone quite smoothly, and Tim was now settled at his new school, with only the occasional nightmare reminding him of the tragic disruption his young life had suffered.

The job itself was proving rather easier than she had expected. Mrs. Petty who came in from the village on an ancient bicycle twice a week turned out to be slipshod but willing, but fortunately, Ginny thought with satisfaction, her new employer was not the type of man to go peering in corners after a few stray cobwebs.

The colour deepened in her face as she thought about Toby Hendrick. He was altogether different from what she had expected. For one thing, he was much younger, and far better looking, with fair hair and smiling blue eyes.

He had arrived at Monk's Dower without giving her any preliminary notice, and the first inkling she had had that the main part of the house was occupied was the gleaming monster of a car parked in the courtyard. She had gone across immediately, her heart sinking. This was her first test as a housekeeper and she'd failed it pretty comprehensively, she thought savagely as she let herself in. His bed wasn't made up, for one thing, and there was no bread or milk in his part of the house, although they had plenty and could share with him.

She was quaking when she arrived in the kitchen and found him on his knees, trying, with a lot of muffled cursing, to get the range going. Ginny had taken over from him, stammering her apologies, but he'd waved them laughingly aside.

"I didn't know I was coming down myself until a few hours ago. I'm a creature of impulse, I'm afraid, Miss...?"

"Clayton," she supplied. "Ginny Clayton."

"Toby Hendrick." He shook hands solemnly with her. "As we're going to be seeing a lot of each other, shall we cut the formality? I'd much rather call you Ginny."

She said, "That's fine with me," letting a curtain of hair fall forward across her face to mask her embarrassment.

No, Toby had certainly not been what she expected. Kathy's descriptive phrase "all man" had prepared her for someone rather different, although she was at a loss to know what. She was glad that the shadowy and rather formidable figure she had built up in her mind was only a figment of her imagination. He certainly wouldn't have been as easy to work for as Toby, she thought, smiling to herself.

And Kathy had been wrong about Vivien Lanyon's interest in him too. She had rung up a couple of times while Ginny was working in the house to make sure that everything was all right, but the exchanges between Toby and herself had been brief and formal in the extreme. Nor had she been over to Monk's Dower, and Ginny told herself that if Mrs. Lanyon had been really interested in Toby, she would never have been away from the door. Perhaps she had decided it was rather degrading to chase a young man who was patently her junior, Ginny thought.

After his first visit, which had lasted only two days, Toby had vanished for three weeks. Then one evening he had telephoned to warn that he would be coming for the weekend, and this time Ginny was fully prepared.

His room was ready, with fresh towels laid out in the adjoining bathroom, and a bowl of early daffodils set on the dressing table. The drawing room fire was lit, and the kitchen range was glowing, while the appetising aroma from a beef stew cooking in its oven crept through the house.

Cooking for Toby did not come within Ginny's official list of duties, but she told herself rather defensively that as she was preparing the stew anyway, it took little effort to put some of the ingredients into a separate casserole. Aunt Mary had raised a caustic eyebrow as she had haltingly tried to explain this, but made no comment.

And Toby's subsequent appreciative remarks had made the extra effort more than worthwhile, she decided smugly before she fell asleep that night. And perhaps it wasn't altogether imagination that the warm gleam in his eyes when he looked at her hadn't simply been prompted by gratitude for the food, delectable though it had been.

Since then he had been down to Monk's Dower every weekend, and Ginny found she was looking forward to each visit with a strange intensity. She knew what was happening to her, of course. She had been vaguely attracted to men before, but it had never meant anything and such relationships as she had enjoyed had been casual in the extreme. But the feeling growing inside her was new to her, and she didn't want to fight it, although common sense told her that she should. After all, she had not the slightest reason to think that Toby felt the same. He looked at her as if the sight of her pleased him, but reason told her that he might well look at any passably attractive girl that way. And he was practically a stranger to her. He worked in London, that much she knew, but she had no idea what he did for a living. She assumed his frequent absences were caused by his trips abroad, but he never mentioned them or any aspect of his life away from Monk's Dower at all.

She sometimes wondered if he had a girl-friend. It was hardly possible that anyone as attractive and charming could still be unattached. She visualised the bleak prospect of his wanting to bring girl-friends down to Monk's Dower with him, as he was perfectly entitled to do, she told herself. How would she feel about that?

There were all kinds of unanswered questions about Toby, she decided. One of the downstairs rooms had been fitted up as a study with a workmanlike desk and a large electric typewriter, but he made no attempt to use it, as far as she knew. Perhaps he went in there and worked during the night—but at what? she wondered.

Surely there was some easy way to find out, without sounding as if she was trying to pry, or get too close. Perhaps this very weekend—if he came down, because the expected message hadn't arrived yet—she would get the opportunity to find out a little more about him, Ginny thought. Maybe he had telephoned while she was out shopping, and was on his way at that moment.

The weekends had begun to assume a kind of pattern. Toby would arrive some time during Friday evening and eat the food that she had left in the oven for him. Then he would come over to their part of the house and join them in their sitting room. Sometimes they would watch television, but at others they would play Scrabble, and Toby had taught Tim how to play gin rummy. He teased Aunt Mary outrageously, and scratched Muffin's stomach with his foot, and behaved pretty much, Ginny thought, as if they were his family, and he had come home.

He was clearly a very social person, and enjoyed the company of others, and Ginny found it strange that he should choose to rent a house in a quiet remote corner like Monk's Dower. She could only surmise that perhaps it presented the greatest possible contrast to his workday life.

On Saturdays he usually got up late and cooked himself an enormous breakfast combined with lunch. Then he went out during the afternoon. Once or twice he had taken Muffin with him for a walk. On another occasion, he had driven Tim into Market Harford and taken him to the cinema.

On the previous weekend, he had taken Ginny herself out for a drive. She'd enjoyed sitting beside him in the big, powerful car. He drove well, she thought judiciously, trying to be objective, but took too many unnecessary risks, relying on his extra speed to get him out of trouble. He hadn't spoken much, and Ginny didn't attempt to break the silence, quite satisfied that he had chosen her company. She hoped secretly that when the afternoon ended he would say, "Don't let's go home yet. I know a place where we can have dinner and dance afterwards."

But he didn't, of course. He just drove her home in the ordinary way. It was dusk as he turned the car through the gates into the courtyard, and the lights were on welcomingly in Ginny's part of the house. She said, trying to sound casual, "Would you like to come in and have some supper with us?"

He turned and looked at her in the gathering darkness, and for a moment she had the oddest feeling that he hadn't been with her at all. Then he smiled and said easily, "Not tonight, Ginny love. I have to get back to town. But I'll be down again soon, so hold my invitation over, will you?"

He helped her out of the car, and she was absurdly conscious of his hand under her arm. She stood very still. Their bodies were almost touching, and if she lifted her face and he lowered his head, their mouths would touch, and she wanted it to happen more than she had ever wanted anything in the world. Something inside her was crying, "Toby, kiss me," so wildly that she was momentarily afraid she might have spoken aloud.

Then the door opened and the light streamed into the courtyard, and the magic moment had gone, and Aunt Mary was calling, "Ginevra, are you there, child?"

She thought she heard Toby mutter something under his breath and hoped very much that it might be a curse of frustration.

He said lightly, "In with you, love. I'll see you."

During the past week, she'd lived on that—the unspoken promise behind, "I'll see you." And the fact that he had called her "love" twice. Surely that must mean something, she thought.

All week she'd hoped that Toby might phone her—not just to say that he was coming for the weekend, and would she have the house ready—but simply to speak to her privately, even if it was just to ask how she was. But the phone had remained inimically silent.

Ginny pressed down on the accelerator, anxious to get home in case there was a message now. As she turned into the lane which led to Monk's Dower, and then on to the Manor, she saw Vivien Lanyon coming towards her on the back of a tall mare. Ginny slowed at once, and pulled in well to her own side of the road. To her surprise, Mrs. Lanyon reined in her horse and dismounted, looping the reins over her arm. Ginny felt a quick flutter of alarm. Over the past weeks she had seen very little of her employer, and she had been quite content for it to be so. She leaned over to the passenger side and wound down her window with some reluctance. Perhaps Vivien Lanyon had decided that Toby was to be her exclusive property after all, and had heard about last weekend's outing. But her employer's expression, though cool, was not particularly unfriendly.

She said, "So there you are. I've been trying to ring you at the house."

"I've been shopping for the weekend's food in Market Harford," Ginny felt obliged to explain. "Tim's at school and Aunt Mary usually has a rest in the afternoons. She doesn't hear the phone from her room when the door's shut."

Vivien Lanyon's brows rose. She said languidly, "Spare me the domestic details. I just wanted to tell you that I've heard from Mr. Hendrick, and he'll be down this weekend. Make sure everything is ready, will you."

She gave Ginny a slight nod, then moved away from the car before re-mounting.

Ginny sat and watched her departure in the rearview mirror. She felt as if she had been abruptly showered with very cold water. So Toby was in contact with Vivien Lanyon after all. Perhaps he liked sophisticated older women. Whatever his tastes, she thought, re-starting the engine with a hand that shook slightly, country mice would come a very poor second each time.

On the other hand, she reasoned as she drove, perhaps he too had been telephoning Monk's Dower and been unable to make Aunt Mary hear, and had phoned Mrs. Lanyon as a last resort. Her spirits rose perceptibly at the thought. And all that really mattered anyway was that he was coming down for the weekend and perhaps this time they would really be alone and no one would interrupt or switch on a light or call out, and he would really kiss her.

Her cheeks were pink and her eyes were bright as she hurriedly unloaded her groceries. The kitchen was full of a

savoury smell. Aunt Mary had been busy making one of
her special chicken casseroles. Ginny decided that she
would wait until Toby arrived and take his helping across to
him in a covered dish. Then the choice was his. He could
either dine in solitary splendour, or come across to their
side of the house and join them for the meal.

She would be very lighthearted and casual about it, she
told herself. She would say laughingly, "I've brought your
supper, but that invitation still stands," and see how he
reacted.

There was a mirror beside the kitchen dresser and she
caught a sudden glimpse of herself, and paused, dissatis-
fied. Why did she have to look so—so damned ordinary?
she asked herself despairingly.

Basically, she could change very little in the time available, but she could at least have a bath and wash her hair.
She had some special cologne she had been saving. She
would use that too.

"He won't know what's hit him," she told the mirrored
reflection defiantly.

Her plans were delayed by the discovery that Muffin had
been sick in the sitting room. She had just finished with the
cloth and disinfectant when Tim arrived in from school,
complaining of imminent starvation, and she sat him down
at the kitchen table with a thick crust cut from the end of a
new loaf indecently loaded with butter, and a glass of milk.

Then Aunt Mary appeared, complaining that she had lost
her reading glasses, and insisting that everyone stop what
they were doing immediately and help her search. The
glasses, safe in their case, eventually came to light down the
side of Aunt Mary's favourite chair in the sitting room,
where she swore she had looked already, and Ginny gave
an unobtrusive look at her watch and smothered a faint
groan. Toby could be arriving at any moment. Her bath
would have to be the quickest dip on record if she was to
complete her chores before his arrival.

Not that it really mattered, she reassured herself as she
ran the water into the bath and tossed in a handful of the

bath salts Tim had given her for Christmas. He would be sharing their supper, so it wouldn't matter if the range wasn't lit. And she would have plenty of time to make up his bed while he was playing cards with Tim.

She towelled her hair briskly, then stroked it dry, using a brush and a hand-dryer. It was still slightly damp as she stood looking through her meagre wardrobe for something to wear. Not a dress, she decided with regret. That would be too obvious altogether, but her best jeans and the white ribbed sweater which made the most of her slender curves. She shook her head and watched her hair swing silkily around her face and was satisfied.

All the time she had been listening for the sound of the engine of his car, but not closely enough, it seemed, for when she went downstairs into the kitchen she saw the car drawn up outside the main door.

She bit her lip vexedly, snatching a handful of cutlery from the drawer and strewing table mats on to the kitchen table at random. She fetched a dish and spooned a helping of the chicken, vegetables and gravy into it, adding potatoes from the pan on top of the stove. It smelled wonderful.

"Almost as good as I do," Ginny said half-aloud, and laughed. She took a last look at herself in the mirror—eyes wide and bright with expectancy, the lines of her mouth softened and vulnerable. She looked more like the child she had been than the woman she wanted to become, but there was nothing she could do about that, and she let herself out of the kitchen door and walked across the courtyard carrying her casserole dish.

It was a cool evening for spring, and the breeze made her shiver a little—or was that only excitement?

She didn't call out as she usually did when she entered the hall at Monk's Dower, but stood listening for a moment. From the kitchen she could hear an exasperated rattling sound, and guessed he was trying to light the range. It was quite simple really—a question of knack, but Toby hadn't mastered it. And he'd be wondering why there was no supper either.

She walked quickly and quietly to the kitchen door, and flung it open. She said gaily, "Surprise—did you..." and stopped, her jaw dropping with shock and fright.

Because the man kneeling in front of the range—the man rising to face her—wasn't Toby at all. He was taller and very dark—dark as a gipsy with a thin arrogant face. He needed a shave and a haircut, and he was wearing faded denims and dark roll-collared sweater which had seen better days, and she registered all these things as if she was seeing them in slow motion, and it was vital that she master every detail.

Ginny was shaking suddenly. The car was here. Toby should be here. Then who was this disreputable-looking stranger?

She said on a high breathless note, "Who are you? And what have you done with Toby?"

She saw him react to that, dark brows drawing together above the thin high-bridged nose, then he moved towards her—one step, that was all—and she was terrified, seeing Toby lying somewhere covered in blood while this man robbed the house.

She heard herself scream something, then she threw the casserole dish straight at his head across the kitchen.

CHAPTER TWO

SHE missed him completely, of course. The casserole whizzed harmlessly past him and shattered on the wall behind him, dropping a nauseous trail of meat and vegetables down the painted plaster. It had been a wasted gesture because it left her without a weapon, and he was still advancing on her. Ginny could almost feel the blaze of anger coming from him, and she looked round instinctively, her eyes falling on the rack of kitchen knives near the sink, every bright blade honed to razor sharpness.

He must have guessed what she was thinking because he said, "Oh, no, you don't, you violent, destructive little bitch!" Before she could move to defend herself, he had vaulted lightly across the pine kitchen table and seized her by the shoulders in a grip which hurt.

"Now then," he said grimly, "who the hell are you, and what are you doing here?"

Dazedly it occurred to her that he didn't sound like a criminal bent on housebreaking—always supposing she had the slightest idea what such a person would sound like. His voice was educated, low and resonant, and if there was menace in it, it was probably sparked off by the fact that he was good and mad.

She said on a sob, "What have you done with Toby?"

"Toby?" he repeated incredulously. "I've done nothing with him, you madwoman. He's in London as far as I know."

"But he was coming down here—I had a message."

He shook his head decisively. "Oh, no, he wasn't. I'd

made it quite clear I'd be using the house myself this weekend. He knows better than to intrude."

"You're the intruder," she gasped. She was shaking now from reaction so violently that if it hadn't been for that bruising grip on her shoulders, she thought she might well have collapsed to the floor at his feet. "You're in his house—you've got his car. Why?"

He swore under his breath. "So that's it." There was a long silence, then he said, "Did Toby tell you this was his house? Answer me, damn you, or I'll break your neck before I break his!"

There was something in his voice, rather than the threatening words themselves, which caught her attention and held it riveted. Panic was filling her up, and a curious sense of unreality. She looked up into his face, absorbing other details—the firm hard lines of his mouth, and his eyes, as cold and grey as a winter sea, and as perilous, she thought wildly.

She marshalled every vestige of self-control of which she was capable in order to say, "Will you let go of me, please. I think there's been a mistake."

"I'm damned sure there has. I still want some answers to my question. Has my feckless cousin been passing off my property as his?"

Ginny said numbly, "Your property?"

He nodded. "Mine. The car certainly—as for the house, I signed the lease and I pay the rent." He looked round the kitchen and his mouth curled derisively. "I also pay a generous service charge. There's supposed to be a housekeeper-caretaker woman living on the premises to keep the place in a permanent state of readiness. If this is a fair sample of the "service" then I'm wasting my money. There aren't even sheets on my bed."

She said on a whisper, "I'm sorry." Her stomach was churning wildly, and she was afraid she was going to be sick. "Do—do you mind telling me your name?"

"It's Hendrick—Max Hendrick." He gave her an impatient glance. "Now do you mind telling me how you come to have the run of the place? Or need I ask? No matter how remote the spot, Toby can always be relied on to organise himself a village maiden." He cast a wry glance at the fragments of broken china, and the remnants of chicken casserole still adhering glutinously to the wall. "And this one can even cook, it seems."

Ginny felt slow hot colour stealing under her skin as she absorbed the implication in his words.

"It isn't what you think."

"No?" He pulled a kitchen chair forward with his foot and motioned her towards it. "So tell me about it."

She moistened her lips frantically. "Toby never actually said he owned the house. I'm afraid I assumed—"

"Altogether too damned much," he cut in abruptly. "Including that you have the right to come and go as you please. Well, you don't, my child. I've rented this place for peace and privacy, and I have no wish for transient female companionship—or at least—"the flick of his eyes over her body was like the lash of a whip"—not the nubile but immature brand you represent. Now if you'd care to clear up the mess you've made, you can go."

She said, "But you must let me explain."

"I don't think any further explanations are necessary," he said. "I'm sorry if you're disappointed about Toby. He should have told you that the house and the car were merely temporary loans while I was abroad."

"It isn't that . . ." she tried again, but he held up a peremptory hand.

"I'd like to cancel any further discussion," he said coolly. "I've been halfway round the world in the past few days, and I've just driven down from London this afternoon, expecting a few home comforts which haven't been provided. I've even had to switch on the immersion heater in the bathroom to obtain enough hot water for a bath. Whatever my so-called caretaker is taking care of, it certainly isn't my interests."

Ginny heard him out, feeling sick. The most galling part of it was that the time she had wasted bathing and prettying herself for Toby had been the time she should have been over in the main part of the house, lighting the kitchen stove, seeing that the water was hot, and making up the bed. Those were the duties she was being paid for, and which she'd failed to carry out, and there was little doubt in her mind that one of the first actions of this angry stranger was going to be to complain to Vivien Lanyon.

Nor had his temper been improved by having a casserole thrown at his head, she thought dejectedly, or by being accused of being an intruder in his own home. There seemed no end to the list of her misdeeds which he could present to Mrs. Lanyon.

She got up from the chair, her mind working madly. There was plenty of chicken left—she could easily fetch another helping. And she could light the range, and make up his bed while he was having his bath. If she did these few basic chores for him, perhaps his temper would cool and he would think twice about complaining about her, she told herself without much conviction.

She said quietly, "I'm sorry you've had such a—poor welcome, Mr. Hendrick. I'll clear up in here before I go."

He nodded curtly, and after giving her one last measuring look he turned and went out of the room.

Hastily Ginny cleaned the mess from the wall and floor, and collected the pieces of broken pottery in a newspaper before depositing them in the kitchen bin. Then she tackled the range, using firelighters and sticks with prodigal recklessness in order to get it going fast. When the fire was burning up well, she rinsed her hands at the sink and started for the door. At the foot of the stairs she paused to remove her shoes, then went upstairs quiet as a cat in her stockinged feet.

The linen cupboard on the landing was well stocked with sheets and pillowcases, and she chose a set at random before tiptoeing across to the door of the master bedroom and listening.

It was quiet, but from the bathroom beyond came the sound of running water. Ginny breathed a sigh of relief as she stepped quietly into the room. The last thing she wanted was another confrontation with the forbidding Mr. Hendrick—not at least until she'd had a chance to put things right. She stripped the covers from the bed and began to make it up, stretching the bottom sheet to an immaculate smoothness with an unsteady hand.

She had behaved like an idiot, she thought miserably. In hindsight, everything pointed to the fact that Toby was not the real tenant, but she had chosen to assume otherwise, and no one had bothered to correct her mistaken impression. After all, her job was to have the house ready for occupation at all times, not to question the identity of the occupier, and Max Hendrick was entitled to lend his house and his car to whomsoever he pleased.

She snatched up a pillow and rammed it into its waiting case with real vindictiveness. It was his own fault if the house wasn't ready for him, she told herself hotly and without pausing to examine her own logic, expecting her to spring into action like a programmed robot through some vague message from a third party. He was cold and arrogant, and she hated him, though she wasn't entirely sure why—unless it was because he couldn't have presented a greater contrast to Toby.

Her newly washed hair flopped across her face as she bent over the bed, tucking in the top sheet, and she pushed it back angrily. She was both disappointed and disillusioned, but the disappointment was paramount. She had built so much on Toby coming down this weekend that this new development was shattering.

But why hadn't Toby told her—warned her? she asked herself almost despairingly. Presumably because he would assume she already knew of his cousin's existence—because unlike Max Hendrick and Vivien Lanyon, he did not regard her simply as a mindless automaton whose sole function was the unquestioning carrying out of orders.

She drew the blankets over the bed, straightening them with small angry jerks, and as she did so became suddenly and paralysingly aware that she was no longer alone.

She straightened slowly and turned apprehensively to

look towards the bathroom. Max Hendrick was standing in its doorway, his hands on his hips. He was smiling a little, but his smile was not pleasant, and as his cold grey eyes went over her Ginny wished suddenly that her jeans did not fit quite so closely to her rounded hips, or her sweater cling quite so revealingly.

He'd shaved, she noticed inconsequentially, so he looked fractionally less like a vagabond, but it was a very small fraction. He still looked dark and dangerous, and the opposite of a conventional tenant for a quiet country house. She remembered Kathy's phrase that he was "all man" and felt at last that she understood what Kathy had meant—although the older woman had presumably never encountered him as Ginny was seeing him now—black hair falling damply across his forehead, and his only covering a towelling bathrobe, opening in a deep vee over the mat of dark hair on his chest, and reaching only to mid-thigh length.

She swallowed nervously, and saw him note her reaction and his amusement deepen.

"What's this?" he asked coolly. "A broad hint that you're not Toby's exclusive property? Do you come with the house, as it were?"

"In a manner of speaking, I suppose I do." Ginny struggled for composure. "But not in the way you obviously think," she added in haste as she saw his brows lift mockingly.

"I'd have said you were the one who was being obvious," he remarked. "I asked you to clear up the mess in the kitchen and leave—yet here you are in my bedroom. And you were clearly all lit up for a weekend of love when you barged in just now," he added, his mouth twisting cynically. "If I've deprived you of your lover's company this weekend, the least I can do is offer you a replacement. I'm sure you'd find me a more than adequate substitute."

He took a step towards her and Ginny recoiled instinctively. The edge of the bed caught her across the back of the legs as she moved, and she collapsed on to it.

"Very flattering," he drawled. "Must it be at once, or can you restrain your feminine ardour until I've eaten?"

"You insulting swine!" Uncaring now of the need to placate him, Ginny levered herself off the bed and faced him, her eyes bright with angry tears. "You have the most monstrous ego of anyone I've ever met in my life! For your information, Toby is not my lover, but even if he were, what makes you think you could ever take his place? As a matter of fact, Mr. Hendrick, I find you not only abominably conceited, but totally resistable as well." She paused for breath. He had halted, and was staring at her, his dark brows dancing together in an ominous frown. "As for being in your bedroom, believe me, it's duty that brings me here, not desire. I'm your housekeeper."

"Oh no, you're not," he said flatly.

"I can assure you I am. If you contact Mrs. Lanyon, she'll confirm it for you."

"I shall be contacting Mrs. Lanyon right enough," he said grimly, "but not to confirm anything."

"What do you mean?" Dismay clutched at her.

"Do I have to spell it out?" he asked rather wearily.

"You mean—you don't want me as your housekeeper?"

"I don't want you in any capacity." His eyes were like ice. "As I mentioned, I've come here for peace and quiet in order to get on with some work. My idea of a housekeeper is someone capable and unobtrusive. You fail on both counts. I can't imagine what possessed Mrs. Lanyon to engage you in the first place."

There was a long silence, then Ginny said with some difficulty, "Mr. Hendrick, I know I've given you a rather poor first impression of my abilities, but—"

"There are no buts," he cut across her incisively. "Even if you carried out your instructions to the letter, I still wouldn't have been prepared to keep you on."

"But that's very unfair," she protested.

"It's an unfair world. Didn't you know?" he returned shortly. "You're young, inexperienced and volatile—and that's a mixture I need like a hole in the head. But don't worry, I'll simply tell Mrs. Lanyon I've been forced to make other arrangements. I won't tell her about the shambles here tonight. You'll get your reference."

She stood staring at him, all the colour drained from her face. Only an hour before, life had been happy and settled. She'd been on top of the world, but now after a few careless words from this man, she was facing disaster again. And if it was only herself, she thought numbly. How was she going to tell Tim and Aunt Mary of this sudden reversal in their fortunes?

Max Hendrick said abruptly, "There's no need to look as if you've seen a ghost. You'll get another job easily enough."

"It isn't the job," she said mechanically "It's the flat—my family. I don't know what we're going to do."

"You have a family?"

"My great-aunt and my young brother. My parents were killed in a road accident three months ago."

He said incredulously, "Are you trying to tell me that you're the breadwinner?"

She said defiantly, her mouth trembling a little, "They're my family. They're all I've got. I—I had to keep us together. That's why a residential job seemed ideal, although the money was poor, but I was going to do some part-time typing to earn extra cash."

Max Hendrick said slowly and very wearily, "Oh, my God!" There was a silence, then he sighed, pushing his hair back from his forehead with an impatient hand. "I'm going to put some clothes on. Go downstairs and wait for me. Make a pot of coffee—strong coffee. You know how to do that?"

She flushed. "Of course, but...."

"As I said before, no 'buts,'" he told her drily. "Can't you even carry out a simple instruction without an argument?"

"Yes," she said, hating him.

"Then prove it." He took her by the shoulders and turned her towards the door.

Her mind was in ferment as she made the coffee. It

seemed by his sudden change of attitude that she might be given another chance. But did she really want one? she asked herself. Was the fragile security they now enjoyed at Monk's Dower really worth the cost of having to work for such an arrogant brute? She sighed, watching the coffee filter through into the jug beneath. Only time would tell—and did she really have a choice, anyway? Could she justify making Tim and Aunt Mary homeless again merely because of a clash of personalities?

She was standing by the window staring into the darkness when he came in. He looked at the jug of black coffee on the table with its attendant cream jug and sugar basin, and the single pottery mug, and his brows rose.

"Won't you join me?"

She shook her head. "Coffee in the evening keeps me awake."

As if she was likely to sleep anyway, she thought bitterly.

He gave a slight shrug, then poured himself some coffee, tasted it and gave a slight nod. "Well, your coffee's drinkable, so that's one point in your favour at least."

"I'm sure all the minuses cancel it out," Ginny said quietly. "I'm sorry the house wasn't ready for your arrival. It—it won't happen again."

"I know it won't," he said in a dry tone. "Because I intend to be here for quite some time. The question is—will you?"

"That's up to you." She would not meet his gaze, but stared down at the quarry-tiled kitchen floor.

"And that's the devil of it," he said, half to himself. He was silent for a moment, then said abruptly, "Tell me about yourself."

Taken aback, she said, "What do you want to know?"

"Anything you care to tell me." He refilled his coffee mug. "I'd like to know primarily why you find yourself in this situation. It isn't every day one comes across someone of your age looking after an old house in a backwater."

"I like housework," she protested. "And I don't have the heavy cleaning to do. Mrs. Petty does that."

"That's hardly the point. You hardly fit the conventional image of a housekeeper." He gave the wall where the casserole had landed a long look. "An Olympic discus thrower, maybe."

"Haven't you heard about the high level of unemployment?" She tried to speak lightly. "You take what you can get and are thankful these days."

"And this was the best you could get?" His glance was quizzical.

"We needed somewhere to live," she said simply. "My father was heavily in debt when he died. Everything had to go, including our home. It isn't easy finding a place when there's a child involved."

"The young brother. How old is he?"

"Eleven. And my great-aunt's in her seventies. She would have—she offered to go into a home, but she'd have hated it. And they wanted to put Tim in care." She felt herself begin to shake at the old remembered nightmare. "I had to find an answer, and this seemed to be it."

"And have you no other family—no one who would have helped?"

"I have an older sister," she admitted, realising with a shock that she had not given Barbie a thought until that moment. "She's an actress. Her new play has just opened in the West End."

"Oh? Which one?"

Ginny wrinkled her nose in an effort to remember. "I think it's called *A Bird in the Hand.*"

"Oh, that one." His tone was neutral; Ginny couldn't figure whether he spoke in praise or blame. "What's your sister's name? What's yours, come to that? I don't think Mrs. Lanyon mentioned it."

"I don't suppose she did," Ginny said wearily. "I'm Ginevra Clayton. My sister's stage name is Barbie Nicholas—it was our mother's maiden name," she added.

"Yours would make a good stage name too."

"If I had any ambitions in that direction—and the talent to go with it, which I haven't."

"No? Then in which direction do your ambitions lie, Miss Ginevra Clayton? I assume you don't mean to spend your days as a junior Mrs. Danvers. Marriage, I suppose, when the right man comes along."

"Perhaps," she said, also trying for a neutral tone, but she failed because involuntarily an image of Toby filled her mind, and the colour flared in her cheeks.

There was a pause, then he said very drily, "The more I hear, the more convinced I am that I should send you packing. Couldn't this sister of yours put you up until you find somewhere?"

"No." Her eyes sought his in dismay, but there was nothing for her comfort in his dark face. There was a remoteness about him, and even a suppressed anger suddenly.

She said in a subdued tone, "I'd better be going. Aunt Mary will be wondering where I am. Shall—shall I finish making your bed before I go?"

"I think I can manage to add the quilt unaided," he said flatly.

"Very well." Ginny lifted her chin. "I'll be over in the morning to see to the fires. Whatever you ultimately decide about me I—I shall continue to carry out the duties I'm being paid for until I leave."

"Bravo," he approved sardonically. "I doubt if even the actress sister could have delivered that little speech without a rehearsal. Perhaps you should reconsider where your talents lie, Ginevra."

It was a shock to hear her name on his lips. Under the circumstances it seemed an unbearable intimacy, and she stiffened. She had never felt so torn. Half of her mind wanted to hang on grimly to what security she had, no matter what the cost. The other half longed to damn him to hell and vanish into the night, never to return. But it was hateful to know that her immediate future depended on his whim.

She forced her lips to move in the semblance of a smile.

"Goodnight, Mr. Hendrick."

"Goodnight," he returned almost absently.

AUNT Mary was waiting in the kitchen, her thin face anxious when Ginny returned.

"My dear child, wherever have you been? Your supper will be ruined. Timothy and I finished long ago."

"It doesn't matter," Ginny assured her almost mechanically. "I—I've been meeting my employer—the new tenant."

Aunt Mary frowned a little. "What are you talking about, my dear? Toby is the tenant."

"Apparently not," Ginny said ruefully. "He's just a cousin who's been allowed to use the place while Mr. Hendrick has been abroad."

"I see. How strange that Toby didn't see fit to acquaint you of the fact."

"I expect he thought it wasn't important." Ginny began on her supper reluctantly. Her appetite seemed to have completely deserted her.

Aunt Mary said, "Hmm," rather sceptically, and busied herself making a fresh pot of tea which she carried over to the table.

"And what's the new tenant like?" she asked, pouring the tea.

"He's an arrogant, unpleasant, unfeeling swine!"

"Ginevra!" her aunt gasped.

"I'm sorry, Aunt Mary." Ginny sounded totally unrepentant. "But you did ask me."

"I gather the gentleman has been unfortunate to arouse your displeasure, and rather early in the acquaintance."

"Whatever he is, he's no gentleman." Ginny's eyes smouldered as she remembered the embarrassment of their encounter in the bedroom. "He didn't believe I was the housekeeper, and when I did convince him, he was damned rude about it." She gave a long, shaky sigh. "Oh, Aunt Mary, I'm afraid I've made such a mess of it all. I—I'm afraid we may have to leave here." And quite suddenly and unexpectedly she laid down her fork and burst into tears.

It was rather like finding that you had slipped back into childhood again. Before many minutes had passed she found rather dazedly that she was upstairs in her room, being put to bed by Aunt Mary. She was tucked in so tightly she could hardly move, a hot water bottle was placed at her feet and a handkerchief smelling of eau de cologne was put gently into her hand. Later, a glass of hot milk appeared which she drank obediently, then, worn out with worry and crying, she fell asleep.

She awoke the following morning later than usual, and exclaimed with horror. She had given her word that she would carry out her duties over at the house, and she was going to be late. She flung on the first clothes which came to hand and raced downstairs. If she followed her usual route across the courtyard, he would see her coming, she thought, but there was another way into the main part of the house. She guessed that once the traditional green baize door had divided the servants' wing from the family rooms, but now the door was a much more solid oaken affair, with a key and bolts on her side only. If she went that way, she might just be able to make Max Hendrick think that she had arrived for work at the correct time.

She felt like a criminal as she unbolted the door and turned the key silently in the lock. Her soft-soled shoes made no noise as she crept along the passage and into the kitchen. Her heart sank a little as she looked round. The room was empty, but the range had been stoked, and there were signs that breakfast had been prepared and cleared away. She had been hoping that Max Hendrick might also have overslept. So where was he now? she wondered. Sitting in that chilly study behind the electric typewriter, wondering why his fire wasn't lit?

She marched along to the study and opened the door after a perfunctory knock. She had a reluctant apology already trembling on her lips, but it was not needed. That room was empty too. She went quietly upstairs and listened, but there wasn't a sound, and when she went over to the landing window and looked out, she realised that the car was gone. He'd got up, had breakfast and gone out. But where? Feeling sick, Ginny thought she could probably guess. He'd gone over to Lanyon Manor to complain about his housekeeper and insist on her replacement. She turned dejectedly away and went downstairs again.

Moving like an automaton, she tidied the kitchen and put his washed dishes away. Then she lit the fire in the study and ran a duster and a carpet sweeper round the room. As she worked, her mind buzzed like a bee trapped behind glass, and with the same desperation.

So it all had to begin again—the weary search for a roof over their heads, for a job with enough money to keep them all. And this time she had no idea even where to start. She supposed dully she would receive a certain amount of notice, or perhaps even money in lieu of notice, if Max Hendrick was really keen to be rid of her as soon as possible. She wondered what kind of reference she would receive, if any. She could not claim to have made a conspicuous success in the job, after all.

She gathered her cleaning materials together and went across the passage into the drawing room. The pale spring sunlight was flooding in through the tall windows, making pools of brightness on the polished floor and the faded Persian carpet. Ginny put the carpet sweeper down and looked around her. She had always liked this room with its spaciousness barely diminished by the big old-fashioned furniture. She walked rather listlessly over to the window to adjust the long brocade curtains, once a rich gold, she thought, but now a uniform beige, and saw that the car had returned.

She thought, "But I didn't hear him come in. How odd," and realised almost at once that it was not odd at all. That she had not heard him because he had not returned to his own part of the house.

She thought furiously, "If he upsets Aunt Mary or Tim..." then threw down her duster and ran out into the hall, and down the passage to the oak door. She could hear the murmur of voices from the kitchen, Tim's voice high with excitement, and Max Hendrick's deeper tones mingling with Aunt Mary's.

Anger rose in her like a hot tide. She flung open the

kitchen door and marched in. The room was warm and full of the aroma of freshly ground coffee. Max Hendrick was sitting at the big table in the centre of the room, very much at his ease, Ginny noticed furiously. Perhaps he felt he had the run of the house, including their part of it, she thought. Well, he would soon find out he was mistaken. She might only have a short time left to live there, but at least she would insist on some privacy for the duration.

"Oh, there you are, dear," Aunt Mary said placidly. "Mr. Hendrick was just asking where you'd got to."

"Really?" Ginny made no effort to conceal the hostility in her voice, and saw Max Hendrick's mouth twist slightly as he studied her. "I was just beginning to wonder the same thing about Mr. Hendrick. You do realise, do you, that our part of the house is supposed to be self-contained? It isn't an extension of your accommodation."

"Ginevra!" Aunt Mary gasped, spilling some of the freshly brewed coffee on to the scrubbed surface of the table in her agitation.

Max Hendrick said coolly, "I apologise for my intrusion on your private domain, Miss Clayton, but I wanted to talk to you fairly urgently. And as we're going to share the house, I thought it would be a good opportunity to introduce myself to the rest of your family."

Ginny felt embarrassed blood pouring into her cheeks as he added drily, "Your great-aunt was kind enough to offer me some coffee. I didn't demand it, if that's what you're thinking."

Ginny subsided abruptly into a chair on the opposite side of the table, fully aware that Tim, who should have been doing his homework, was absorbing the little drama open-mouthed.

She said, more sharply than she intended, "You can't possibly concentrate on your maths if we're going to talk, Tim. Take your books up to your room, please."

When the door had closed behind Tim's lagging figure, Max Hendrick said pleasantly, "Are you always so dismissive with him? He'll be growing up soon, you know."

"Yes, I do know, thank you," she said stonily. "Actually he's still quite a little boy in many ways. He had a lot of bad dreams after—after the accident, but they seem to have subsided since we came here. I—I don't want him to hear anything which might upset him, and start the nightmares off again."

Max Hendrick said bitingly, "I'm not an ogre, and I don't make a habit of going round deliberately upsetting children— even those of your age." He stood up, swallowing down the coffee that remained in his cup. "I came here this morning because I had a proposition to put to you. I've outlined it to your aunt, so she can give you the details. I'd like an answer as soon as possible, please." He gave her a curt nod and turned away towards the door with Aunt Mary, clearly distressed, in attendance.

Ginny sipped her coffee, but it tasted oddly bitter and she pushed the cup away with a slight grimace as Aunt Mary came back.

"My dear child, whatever possessed you to be so abominably rude?"

Ginny sighed. "I suppose I was rude, but I couldn't help it. I just don't like him. He's so cold and hard and arrogant. In fact, I can hardly believe that he's Toby's cousin. There's not even a family resemblance."

"Ah, yes, Toby," Aunt Mary said vaguely. "So surprising that he never mentioned . . . but there. I'm sorry you dislike Mr. Hendrick so much, Ginevra. I found him quite charming."

Ginny forced a smile. "He doesn't bother to waste his charm on me, Aunt Mary. Our aversion is quite mutual, I promise you. What is this proposition he has for me? A housekeeping job in the Shetland Islands?"

"On the contrary." Aunt Mary sat down at the table and poured herself some more coffee. "Apparently you mentioned last night that you propose to supplement your income with some part-time typing."

"Did I?" Ginny racked her brain to remember. Other things returned with appalling clarity, but not that particular incident.

"Apparently, yes." Her aunt's tone was dry. "It seems Mr. Hendrick needs the services of a secretary himself, and he came here this morning to offer you the job."

Ginny sat very still, as if she had been frozen. Then she shook her head very slowly. "It can't be true," she said. "He doesn't want me to work for him. He said so last night. I was sure he'd gone to the Manor this morning to tell Mrs. Lanyon that he was giving me notice."

"He went to the Manor to hire a horse so that he can ride each morning while he's here," Aunt Mary said briskly. "And he clearly has no intention of giving you notice."

"No," Ginny said numbly. She still found it difficult to credit what she had been told. She had been sure—so sure that Max Hendrick didn't want her working for him in any capacity. And now he was offering her the chance to become his secretary. She thought of the modern efficiency of the big typewriter which sat like an alien in the panelled study. She thought of having to share that room with Max Hendrick, of transcribing the notes and letters he dictated to her under his watchful gaze. She gave a slight shiver.

"His offer is a real blessing," Aunt Mary said happily. "It couldn't have come at a better time either. The first quarter's bills will soon be arriving, and there's Tim's trip to consider."

"Trip?" Ginny queried, trying to make herself think coherently.

"Yes, dear. A school visit to France at the beginning of the summer holidays. He deliberately didn't mention it to you because he knew how little money there was even for essentials, but nearly all his classmates will be going, and I thought that if I contributed towards the cost as well, perhaps we would be able to send him."

"But I don't want to work for Max Hendrick," Ginny burst out, dismayed. "I told you, Aunt Mary, I don't like the man. If I take this job I'll have to see him every day. I'll have no choice—unless he uses a dictaphone, and I haven't seen one around." She broke off despairingly, seeing Aunt Mary's lips tighten in incomprehension and disapproval. "You think I'm being ridiculous—hysterical."

"I can't understand you, Ginevra. You need work—exactly the sort of work that Mr. Hendrick has offered you. Can you be sure that any other potential employer would be any more to your taste?"

"No," Ginny admitted. "But at least I'll be sure that they won't be offering me work out of some misplaced sense of charity." She was angry now, both with herself for having told Max Hendrick so much about their personal circumstances and with him for having regarded her unthinking outburst as a cry for help. She said, "Max Hendrick and I are better apart, believe me."

"After your behaviour this morning, he may well share your sentiments," said Aunt Mary, her back very straight. 'It was kind of him not to withdraw the offer."

Kind, thought Ginny. Is that how it seems to her? But he's not a kind man. She remembered how his hands had hurt her, the coldness of his eyes and mouth, his insulting assumptions about her motives for being in his bedroom, and her relationship with Toby. There'd been no kindness about him then. Nor was there now, she thought. This offer had been made with a kind of exasperated pity, dredged out of him because she'd been fool enough to inflict her problems upon him. He'd made it, no doubt, out of a sense of unwilling obligation, but honour was satisfied now, and her refusal could only be a relief to them both.

She rose determinedly. "I'll go and see him now," she said.

She was disgusted to find that she was trembling a little as she knocked at the study door, and the note of impatience in his voice as he told her to enter did nothing to restore her composure.

The study wasn't nearly as tidy as she had left it. The desk top was littered with papers and documents and Max Hendrick was studying a thick file which was open in front of him. The typewriter, she noticed, had been moved to a side table under the window. So she would have been expected to work in the same room. The knowledge hardened her resolve.

"Well, go on, Ginevra." He tossed the file down on the desk and leaned back in his chair. "Turn me down."

She was nonplussed for a moment. "How did you know?"

"It didn't need clairvoyant powers," he said coolly. "Apart from the look of apprehension as you came in, you're very predictable. But I did think that expediency might triumph over your natural desire to tell me to go to hell and take my job with me."

"I hardly see where expediency comes into it," she said.

"No?" He raised his brows. "Your great-aunt was quite frank with me, you know. She's worried sick about you and the amount of responsibility you've taken on. I thought you might have been perceptive enough to see how she felt, and done something to alleviate her worries."

"And working for you is the only answer, of course."

"It might well be," he said slowly. "This is the local paper. I bought it this morning. There are at least a dozen hopefuls offering a home typing service, and very little in the Situations Vacant column. Even in this backwater you have to compete, it seems."

"I'll manage," she said defiantly. She lifted her chin and stared at him. "I swear I'll manage."

"At the expense of your aunt's peace of mind?" he asked with an ironic smile. "Where are you going to find the money for the electricity account, or the telephone bill, not to mention your brother's school trip? He was full of it before you came in. Pity to disappoint him."

"He won't be disappointed," Ginny said obstinately, inwardly furious that he knew so much about them.

"No? You expect to find the money from the wages you're paid to look after this place? My God, they're barely enough to feed and clothe you!" He got up, pushing back his chair, and came round to where she stood. "Don't be a little fool, Ginny. You need this job, and you know it. All right, so you don't want to work for me. I can accept that. You wouldn't be my ideal choice either, but at least you're on the spot. I'm assuming that your shorthand and typing are competent, and I'm promising that they'll have to be—

come more than that. I have high standards, and you'll earn
every penny that you're paid."

"You talk as if the choice was no longer mine."

"I'm not sure that it is." He paused, then said harshly,
"If you're harbouring any secret fears that I see you in anything but a purely professional light, then forget it. I'll make
demands on your secretarial abilities, but that's all."

"It never entered my head," she said haughtily.

"No?" He smiled grimly. "You have a short memory,
my sweet. Last night you seemed to think rape was not only
imminent but inevitable."

Ginny was silent, loathing him for reminding her.

"I'd like you to start on Monday," he said, after a
pause. "Ten o'clock seems a reasonable hour to begin.
Agreed?"

She wanted to refuse quite desperately. He was standing
so close to her that their bodies were almost touching. If he
moved even slightly, he would brush against her. She
wanted to step back, away from him, but to do so would be
an admission of weakness, an acknowledgement of her
awareness of him. And that was something she didn't even
want to acknowledge to herself.

She said unhappily, "I don't even know the sort of work
you want me to do. Is it letters—reports?"

"No," he shook his head. "Scripts—dialogue. I'm a playwright."

She was startled into meeting his gaze. There always had
been something vaguely familiar about his name, she
thought, but the shock of his arrival and its subsequent re-
percussions had driven it from her mind.

"Are you well-known?" she asked naïvely, and saw
him smile briefly.

"Fairly," he said. "Does this sudden interest in my career mean you're going to work for me?"

Her mouth twisted bitterly. "You're quite right. I don't
really have a choice. And—and I have to think of Tim and
my aunt."

"There might even come a day when you'll be able to

think of yourself," he said. He put out a casual hand and tilted her chin up towards him. She felt herself go rigid.

"Just testing," he said smoothly, and released her. "You don't like my touching you, do you?"

"I may have to work for you, Mr. Hendrick," she said between her teeth, "but that doesn't mean I have to like anything about you."

He threw back his head and laughed.

"Cheer up, Ginevra," he said. "Remember the old saying—Better the devil you know.... And if you're a good girl and work hard, I might even give you a bonus and invite Toby down for the weekend."

Ginny felt the betraying colour slide into her face, knew that she was vulnerable and defenceless as if she had been naked under his mocking glance.

She said in a low furious voice, "Damn you to hell, Max Hendrick," then whirled and ran out of the room.

CHAPTER THREE

GINNY spent a miserable weekend. Even Aunt Mary's relief at her change of heart and Tim's open jubilation could not reconcile her to the prospect of Monday morning.

And one of Barbie's infrequent phone calls was the last straw. Her sister was clearly in a bad temper. The play had opened in the North to very mixed notices and it seemed a major re-think had to take place if they were ever going to reach the West End.

But even Ginny had not expected her reaction when she diffidently mentioned her new job.

"You're going to work for Max Hendrick?" Barbara had repeated with utter incredulity. "You can't be serious! He's out in California."

"He may well have been," Ginny said rather wearily. "But he's here at Monk's Dower now."

"My God!" Barbara digested this in silence for a moment. Then she said almost absently, "It's the chance of a lifetime."

"Hardly," said Ginny. "I don't even like him. I wish he'd stayed in California."

"Don't be a fool," Barbara snapped. "You don't really know who he is, do you?"

"He says he's a playwright. And I thought I knew the name...."

"God, you're an imbecile!" Ginny flinched at the contempt in her sister's voice. "He says he's a playwright, indeed! He didn't mention the fact that he's had a string of West End hits, all of which have transferred to Broadway? He didn't mention the awards he's won, and the film rights he's sold?"

"No, he didn't," Ginny said, chastened.

"Of course he didn't. He'd expect you to know. Everyone in the world but you must have heard of Max Hendrick. And you're going to be his secretary!" Barbara gave an almost strident laugh. "And I'm stuck here hundreds of miles away!"

Ginny tried to make bewildered sense of what she was saying. "But you couldn't work for him, Barbie. You can't even type and...."

"Who said anything about typing?" Barbara almost wailed. "Everyone knows that Max Hendrick has a say in the casting of all his plays. If I met him—made an impression—then he might remember me at the next audition. I know you know nothing about the theatre, but surely you can see that."

Ginny said unhappily, "Perhaps—but I'm not sure it would be all that easy to make an impression on him—a lasting one, that is."

"Just as long as it lasted until the next auditions for his new play," said Barbara. "What's the matter, ducky? You sound a bit jaundiced. You didn't hope to make an impression, I trust. The lovely Mr. Hendrick is quite out of your league. He can have any woman he wants, and frequently does by all accounts."

Ginny said sharply, "He doesn't interest me in that way in the slightest."

"Just as well," Barbara said negligently. "Because you certainly wouldn't interest him. That's probably why he offered you the job—he likes to keep his business and private lives strictly apart."

"Very probably," Ginny agreed, strictly repressing the memory of herself outstretched and helpless across Max Hendrick's bed.

"I should have a weekend free pretty soon," Barbara said abruptly. "They'll have to do something drastic to knock this disaster into shape if it's going to be taken into London. I might pay you a visit. I presume you have a spare room?"

Ginny's heart sank. "Not really," she said. "But there's a spare bed in my room."

"Well, that will have to do, I suppose. You could sound a little more enthusiastic at the prospect."

"It's just that—" Ginny felt her way carefully. "Barbie, you will remember that he's my employer, won't you?"

"Darling," Barbie sounded amused, "I shall have the greatest difficulty in remembering anything else! See you soon." And she rang off.

Ginny replaced her own receiver, conscious of an acute feeling of depression. Barbara at Monk's Dower making an impression on Max Hendrick was a complication her life could well do without, she thought.

Sunday passed relatively quietly. Ginny signed the form Tim had brought home from school about the trip, and felt that the die had somehow been cast. She would make a success of this job, she told herself fiercely, in spite of the clash of personalities between herself and Max Hendrick. It represented security and that was all that mattered. That was all that had to matter.

Monday morning was also Mrs. Petty's day, and she was already at work scrubbing the kitchen floor when Ginny arrived to make sure everything was in order.

"He's come, then," Mrs. Petty remarked comfortably, squeezing out her floor cloth. She gave Ginny a broad wink. "I daresay her ladyship will be camping on the doorstep soon."

With a start, Ginny realised she had forgotten about Vivien Lanyon. She had thought her rather hard-looking but undeniably attractive and a woman of the world to her fingertips. She guessed that she and Max Hendrick would be about the same age too, and remembered Kathy's friendly warning.

She parried Mrs. Petty's inquisitive remarks and made a tray of coffee which she carried along to the study. She knocked and waited.

The door was flung open so abruptly that she started, nearly spilling the coffee, and Max towered over her.

"Let's get one thing straight, shall we," he said without preamble. "While you're working for me, you enter this room without knocking. I don't want my concentration disturbed by having to shout "Come in" every five minutes. And I hope you can drink that coffee while you work. I don't break during the morning except for lunch."

"I see." Ginny set the tray down on the desk, inwardly seething.

"Even if you don't, you soon will," he said as he resumed his seat.

She carried her own mug over to the typewriter by the window, and looked down in consternation at the pile of handwritten sheets awaiting her transcription.

"What's the matter?" Max demanded impatiently.

She swallowed. "I hope I can read your writing."

"Let's both hope so." He nodded at the typewriter. "Ever used one of those?"

"Not this particular model," she admitted. She looked round. "Where do you keep the paper and carbons?"

"In the cupboard," he said. "That's your responsibility. You'd better chase up the nearest wholesaler and make sure they're prepared to deliver fresh supplies as and when they're needed. If you run out, I shan't be amused. Now then—" He pulled a sheet of paper towards him and quickly sketched out how he wanted each completed page to look, then gave precise instructions about the number of carbons he required, and other relevant details. Ginny was stiff with tension by the time he'd finished, glad to be able to sink down on to her own chair and turn her back on him. She ran a frantic eye over the keyboard as she assembled her first set of sheets. She would have liked some time to familiarise herself with it rather than have to start working immediately. She was bound to make mistakes, she thought miserably as she adjusted the tabulator minutely.

And mistakes she made.

As she discarded yet another set of ruined pages, cursing under her breath, Max said rather wearily, "We're going to need that wholesaler sooner than I thought."

A flush rose in her cheeks. "I'm sorry, I'm rather nervous. I'm not used to being watched while I work."

"Then you'll have to get used to it," he said pleasantly. "And the sooner the better."

She'd been on the point of asking him if she could move the typewriter and other paraphernalia into another room—perhaps even organise one of the unused bedrooms upstairs into an office for herself, but his comment seemed to kill the request stone dead. Ginny gritted her teeth and struggled on, while the forgotten coffee congealed beside her.

She felt as limp as a rag when he announced abruptly that it was lunchtime, and very close to tears. She was normally a good typist, but this morning her fingers had all been thumbs, and someone else's thumbs at that. Her pile of completed typescript looked pitifully thin, and she could tell Max thought so too as she saw him glancing at it, his eyebrows raised slightly. He gave her a frowning look.

"For God's sake, relax," he said. "What's eating you?"

She shrugged. "It's all so unfamiliar. And I didn't realise just how famous you were. You must have thought I was an awful fool."

"Because you hadn't heard of me?" He looked faintly amused. "I'm not that conceited, Ginevra. And I doubt whether the fact that I'm better known than you thought has made me any more acceptable to you. You have an extraordinarily expressive face—and an equally expressive back. I still think it's a pity you didn't try for a career on the stage."

"One of us is quite enough."

"Oh, yes, the sister," he nodded. "Did she tell you all about me?"

She flushed rather defensively. "As a matter of fact, she did."

His smile widened. "And told you off because you hadn't recognised my name for yourself?"

Off guard, she said, "How did you know . . ." and stopped.

"A lifetime's acquaintance with young actresses," he said drily. "What's she like, this sister?"

"Beautiful," Ginny said baldly.

"That isn't usually enough. Not these days. Is she talented as well?"

Ginny shrugged again. "I suppose she must be. She gets a lot of work."

"Does she now." He was silent for a moment. "Can you really be as innocent as you sound?"

"I don't know what you mean."

"No?" He studied her face for a moment, noting her widening eyes, the flush still lingering on her cheekbones, and gave a short harsh sigh. "No, probably you don't. Forget it, Ginevra, and go and have some lunch. Be back at two, please."

Oddly enough, when she returned after her snack of soup and sandwiches, things were easier. Her errors became fewer and her natural rhythm began to return. She was still conscious of Max's presence, of course, but not all the time. By the end of the afternoon it was only a movement, or the creak of his chair, or the click of his lighter as he lit one of the long black cheroots he smoked that reminded her she was not alone.

The work she was doing interested her too. The only plays she had read in her life had been at school, and she had not cared for the rigidity of the classroom readings, or the cut-and-dried interpretations of character and motive which the teachers had imposed. Now she began to discover for herself the art of maintaining tension and revealing character through dialogue, and a quiet fascination laid hold of her. She was almost startled when Max said, "That's it for today."

"I'll just finish this page," she said.

"Leave it." He lifted an eyebrow. "Unless you're angling for overtime."

"I'd never even considered it," she denied indignantly.

"Yes, I absolve you of that. You haven't even enquired what I'm going to pay you. You're very trusting, Ginevra. You could find you were working for love."

She couldn't repress the swift, startled look she gave him, and his mouth twisted wryly.

"It's a good thing I don't harbour any illusions that I'm irresistible," he commented. "You'd soon teach me very different, wouldn't you?"

"I don't think I could teach you anything at all." She had risen from her chair and was standing beside it, holding herself stiffly, conscious of a need for defence. She swallowed. "You implied that this was strictly a business relationship. If that's the case, then can we please avoid these—personal conversations. They don't amuse me—and they oughtn't to amuse you. I'm not a worthy opponent, Mr. Hendrick."

"Point taken." He sat down on the edge of the desk, thrusting his hands into the pockets of his slacks. "Let's get back to business, then." He named the weekly sum he proposed to pay her, and she gaped at him.

"But that's ridiculous!" she burst out. "It's twice what I was getting in my last job."

"Don't speak too soon," he said drily. "You may find you're working twice as hard. I've been told I'm a slave-driver, especially when I hit a snag. But those are my terms, take them or leave them."

"You're very generous," she said in a subdued voice.

"No," he said. "You'll find that I expect my pound of flesh in return, and more than that at times. Not—"his eyes slid over her"—that there's a pound to spare on you—or does that come within the category of unacceptable personal conversation?"

"Probably," she said. "You really think I'm an idiot, don't you?"

"I think you're very young." His tone was unrevealing. "But I'm used to having a fairly close relationship with my secretaries. It's going to take time to adjust. You'll have to make allowances if I forget sometimes and treat you like a normal young woman instead of a novice nun."

As she went back to her own part of the house, Ginny found herself wondering about his previous secretaries. "Close," he'd said. But did he mean friendly or intimate? Not that it mattered to her, she hastened to assure herself. As long as he kept his distance with her, she had nothing to worry about. Yet she was curiously preoccupied as she helped prepare the evening meal, and found herself answering Aunt Mary's questions about her day rather at random.

She approached her second day as Max's secretary with far less foreboding than she had the first. He wasn't in the study when she arrived, and she wondered if he had gone over to the Manor again. She supposed she was intended to get on with the typing and slid into her chair, reaching for the coloured folder in which she had placed her completed sheets.

She took one look at them, and an exclamation of dismay escaped her lips. Lines had been altered on every page, sections of dialogue had been transposed, and even one character's name had been changed. It was all to do again, she thought turning over the sheets in desperation. With a heavy sigh she reached for paper and carbons. This must be part of the pound of flesh which Max had mentioned, she told herself dispiritedly.

She was concentrating so determinedly that she didn't hear the car return. The slam of the front door made her jump, and then she was aware of Max's long stride coming down the passage. As he entered, he gave her an unsmiling "Good morning" and went to his desk.

She returned his greeting quietly and applied herself even more ferociously to her work. After a pause, he said, "I see you found the alterations."

"That's putting it mildly," she muttered. "Do you intend to do this with every scene you write?"

"If it needs it, yes," he drawled. "Any objections?"

"Certainly not. You pay me to type, not to object. But if this is how you operate, then progress is going to be slow."

"Yes, this is how I operate," he said. "And progress will be just as fast as it needs to be, Miss Ginevra Clayton. I'm writing to a deadline, and we'll work together here all night as the deadline approaches if necessary. Sure you can cope?"

The dark eyes seemed to flare a challenge at her, and she

was strongly tempted to hang her head and confess that she didn't think she could cope at all. This was a far cry from the sort of home typing job she had envisaged. Letters, she thought, for people whose businesses were too small to allow them to employ someone full-time. Theses for students, perhaps and—yes—manuscripts for hopeful authors. She'd considered all these possibilities. But the kind of demands that Max Hendrick might make of her she had not foreseen at all, she thought, dismayed. And the pressure was only just beginning.

She said with an assurance that was wholly assumed, "Of course I can cope, Mr. Hendrick."

"Good," he said unemotionally. "And I'd be grateful if you'd drop the formality. I'd prefer you to call me Max."

"Did all your other secretaries use your first name?"

"Without argument or hesitation. You, Ginevra, seem to be in a class of your own."

"You said it would take you time to adjust. Can't you make the same allowances for me?"

"I don't really have to make any allowances at all. I pay the piper, and I should be able to call the tune."

She said in a stifled tone, "Yes, you should. I was forgetting."

"And none of my other secretaries managed to make me feel guilty either. You're scoring a lot of firsts, Ginny Clayton."

She was tense again, and the speed and rhythm of her typing faltered accordingly. She forced herself to proceed steadily and carefully, and avoid the sort of mistakes she had made the previous day. By the time her morning's work was done, her shoulders ached and she felt as taut as a violin string.

As she went towards the door Max said abruptly, "I need you to do me a favour."

"Extra work?"

"Of a sort. I'm giving a small dinner party on Friday evening, and I would like you to do the cooking for it, if you are willing. I'd pay you, of course."

Ginny said, "But how do you know I can cook?" As soon as the words were uttered, she found herself colouring a little. "Oh—Toby, I suppose."

"Yes, Toby." He gave her a sardonic look. "Other and rather more significant details he omitted to mention."

She gave a slight shake of her head. "I don't think I'd be capable of cooking for a dinner party."

"I don't want anything too elaborate. A good casserole perhaps as the main course, with grapefruit to start and a syllabub as dessert. Could you manage that?"

"How many guests are you expecting?"

"Only one," he said. "Mrs. Lanyon."

She said stonily, "Then I can't very well refuse, can I?"

"Yes, you can quite easily," he said. "But I hope you won't. Please do this thing for me, Ginny. I promise I won't make a habit of asking you."

Ginny agreed tonelessly. As she ate her lunch, she wondered when the invitation had been issued. Probably that morning, she thought, and that was why he had been late back from his early morning ride. Mrs. Lanyon, it seemed, had lost no time in staking a claim to her new tenant. She remembered Kathy's remark, "She marked him down as hers the moment she laid eyes on him."

Ginny thought, "She's welcome to him. They're welcome to each other."

As the week approached its end she thought that she had never been so tired in her life, getting up early in the morning to attend to all the necessary chores, then speeding back to her own wing of the house to wash and change and gulp down some breakfast before presenting herself in the study. Each day there were corrections of the work she had done the previous day to deal with, and each day she felt that faint spirit of rebellion as she saw the destruction of her neatly typed pages, but gradually as the first act began to take shape before her eyes, she had to concede that Max knew exactly what he was about. She could not complain about his attitude towards her either. His manner was pleasant, but faintly aloof, and she told herself defiantly that she was glad of this. It meant that she could concentrate on the work she was being paid for without being constantly on edge, wondering how to counter his next remark.

She was given Friday morning off so that she could go into Market Harford and buy what she needed for the evening meal. Mrs. Petty had arrived and been set, not without some sotto voce grumbling, to cleaning a pair of silver candlesticks which Ginny had discovered in a cupboard in the dining room. There would be flowers to get, she thought, sitting at the kitchen table over a cup of coffee while she made her list, and tall candles—red ones, she decided, visualising the dining room with its polished mahogany furniture and floor-length crimson brocade curtains. A candlelit dinner for two with everything that implied.

She suffered an odd little pang at the thought and the words on her list blurred and grew meaningless for a moment. She was missing Toby, she thought rather desolately, and the worst of it was she had no idea when, if ever, he would be coming down to Monk's Dower again. She bit her lip angrily as she remembered Max's cynical remark about inviting him. It hadn't been mentioned since, she thought. Probably Max would disapprove of his cousin becoming involved with the hired help. Apart from anything else, he wouldn't want her mind being distracted from the job in hand, although he permitted himself such distractions. She jabbed her pencil into the sheet of paper in front of her so viciously that the point broke.

Muffin barking vigorously at the kitchen door aroused her from her resentful reverie, and she was surprised to see the postman approaching. Since they had moved to Monk's Dower they had received few letters. Perhaps the morning mail was bringing one of the quarterly bills she was beginning to dread.

Or could it be a letter from Toby? Was that why the image of him had suddenly been so strong in her mind? Her heart was beating painfully as she answered the door. However, it wasn't a letter, but a bulky packet. The postmark was London, and the large rather flamboyant printing of the address was unmistakably Barbara's.

Ginny frowned a little as she slit the packet carefully open. It was nowhere near her birthday, although no one would be less likely to remember than Barbara if it was, and she was a notoriously poor correspondent. The outer wrappings revealed a layer of corrugated cardboard and when this was removed, Ginny found herself holding a flat leather folder.

She opened it slowly. It was a photograph, of course. One of the glamorous head-and-shoulders shot used for publicity purposes, and signed ostentatiously, "All my love, darlings, Barbie."

Ginny stared down at it, utterly bewildered. What on earth had possessed Barbara to send such a thing? she asked herself. It was far from being a typical portrait for the family album. It had been taken in soft focus, and it made Barbie's eyes look larger than ever and more luminous, her mouth soft and full and pouting slightly. Her arms and shoulders were bare, and though the photograph discreetly stopped at her shadowy cleavage, nevertheless it managed to give the disturbing impression that she had been totally nude when it was taken.

Ginny thought, "It's quite deliberate. It's the pose, the look in her eyes, everything." The invitation was quite blatant and Ginny was conscious of a feeling of distaste. It seemed totally out of place in this small homely kitchen in the heart of the country—like an orchid in a vegetable rack, Ginny thought, or one of those horrid exotic plants which ate things.

She went hot and cold all over, closing the folder and putting it down on the table as if it had burned her fingers. She knew, of course, why Barbara had sent it. It might have been addressed to Ginny, but it was intended for Max Hendrick. She was intended, she supposed, to display it somewhere where he would notice it. And his attention, once caught, would be riveted when Barbara herself arrived on the scene.

Ginny gathered up the discarded wrappings with fingers

that trembled slightly and thrust them into the kitchen bin. She would dearly have liked to include the photograph as well, but she knew that would only involve her in difficulties when Barbara did arrive.

And her sister was beautiful, she thought, opening the folder and studying the picture with troubled eyes. Beautiful and ambitious and ruthlessly single-minded when it came to her career.

She found herself remembering what Barbara had said about Max Hendrick. "*He can have any woman he wants, and frequently does, by all accounts.*" Was the photograph a visual message signifying that he could have her too, if he wished?

Ginny shivered. Max had said she was innocent, and they'd been talking about Barbie. She moved in a world which Max knew well, and he would have no difficulty in reading the signal this photograph was sending. If he saw it, that was, and Ginny had no intention of letting him see it. She would put it upstairs in her own room, away from everyone, and if Barbara was angry, she would protest that she had misunderstood.

She found another pencil and wrote "red candles" on her list, reflecting as she did so that if Max was becoming involved with Vivien Lanyon then he would have little time in his life for Barbie. But for some reason it was not a particularly consoling thought, and Ginny had a strong premonition that there were stormy times ahead as she set out for Market Harford.

The only item on the list which caused her any problems was the candles, but eventually she tracked them down in a gift shop in the market square. She had just emerged and was on her way back to the car when someone called out to her. She turned and saw it was Kathy.

"Thought it was you," Kathy greeted her amiably. "I wondered if you'd got time for a coffee." She sensed Ginny's hesitation and added, "But if you'd rather not...."

"It isn't that," Ginny hastened to assure her. "I'd love some coffee, but I mustn't be too long because I've got

some steak that needs long slow cooking for this evening."
She paused, and said awkwardly, "Mrs. Lanyon is coming
to dinner, and I need to make a good impression."

"Told you she was after him," Kathy remarked, as they
made their way to the little café on the other side of the
square. "Didn't take long, did it? And I wouldn't worry too
much about the dinner, if I were you. She'll have her mind
on the afters." She chuckled. "You could probably serve up
bedsocks in aspic and she wouldn't notice."

Ginny's own smile was rather constrained. As they sat
down at a corner table, Kathy gave her a critical look.

"You're looking tired," she remarked forthrightly. "And
you've lost some weight, if I'm not mistaken. Job too much
for you, is it?"

"Oh, no, it's fine," Ginny said hastily. Kathy appeared
friendly enough, but she didn't want word going back to the
Manor that she was unable to cope. That was one reason
why she wanted so desperately for tonight's dinner party to
be a success—to underline the fact that she could cope
more than efficiently. "I—I'm working as Mr. Hendrick's
secretary as well."

"Are you now?" Kathy took a battered packet of cigarettes from her bag and offered one to Ginny before lighting her own. "Does Madam know?"

Ginny was slightly disconcerted. "I imagine she does. I
thought he would have told her. After all, he comes over to
the Manor to ride each morning."

"Well, maybe he has." Kathy's tone made it clear that she
considered this doubtful in the extreme. "Just remember
what I told you. No poaching on her ladyship's preserves if
you value your job. Which reminds me—"she paused while
the waitress brought them their coffee and a plate of bis-
cuits"—is that shaggy brown-haired mongrel yours?"

"Yes." Ginny added sugar to her coffee. "Well, he belongs to my young brother, actually. Why do you ask?"

"Let him out during the day, do you?" Kathy added a
swirl of cream to her own cup.

"Not usually." Ginny remembered Aunt Mary complaining that Muffin had run off a couple of times when she had let him out, and had returned much later covered in mud. "I think he goes rabbiting sometimes."

"As long as that's all it is." Kathy took a biscuit. "More used to town life, is he?"

"Yes," Ginny smiled. "The country must seem like paradise to him."

"It probably does," Kathy nodded. "But in its own way it can be more dangerous than the town. You want to keep an eye on him."

Ginny was puzzled. "You think he might get hurt in some way?"

"He might—or he might end up doing the hurting, which would be worse. The Hendersons at the Home Farm were complaining that a dog had got in among their hens the other day and was chasing them all over the place. He didn't catch one, but it put them off their laying, and Mrs. Henderson wasn't best pleased, I can tell you. Luckily she spoke to me about it and not to Madam, otherwise you'd have heard more and sooner."

"Oh, lord!" Ginny was dismayed. "But he was only playing with them, surely. He wouldn't have intended any harm. He's a family pet and very good-natured."

"Even the best-natured dog can change—if he gets a taste for blood." Kathy's voice was dry. "I'd keep him in if I were you, and make sure your brother puts him on a lead when he takes him out. Better to be safe than sorry, wouldn't you agree?"

Ginny said, "Yes," rather numbly. The black cloud which the arrival of the photograph had caused to gather over her head seemed to be increasing. All she would need to do now was ruin the dinner, she thought ruefully.

She was glad when the subject changed to rather more cheerful topics. Kathy was a mine of information on the local social events, but as many of her anecdotes depended on personal knowledge of the people involved some of the point of what she was saying was lost on Ginny.

"You need to get out more, ducky," she boomed cheerfully. "Meet people—get to know some young men. All work and no play, you know."

Ginny forced a smile. "I think I'm already rather a dull girl," she said lightly. "And I don't really have a great deal of time to spend on myself." She didn't add that sometimes after clearing away the evening meal, dealing with whatever laundry had accrued, and chivvying Tim over his homework, she found herself falling asleep in her armchair with Aunt Mary's precise tones discussing the events of the day forming a convenient lullaby.

It was dull, she thought with sudden dissatisfaction, and she was dull too, and probably Toby thought so too and wouldn't come down again, even if he was asked, and all the promise she'd inferred from his words had been sheer imagination. Probably the only excitement she had to look forward to was the unpleasant verbal sparring which Max had subjected her to, and even that seemed to have died the death.

She was rather glad she could use the excuse of the evening meal to make an early departure. Kathy was a cheerful soul, she thought as she drove back to Monk's Dower, yet nearly everything she had said had contrived to depress her. She was turning into a cabbage, she thought, and allowing Muffin to riot unchecked round the countryside. The only thing she might have argued with was the idea of her being a possible rival to Vivien Lanyon.

Nothing, Ginny told herself, could be further from the truth. She could reluctantly concede that Max Hendrick was attractive, or would be to the majority of women, but she was not among them. Max was something of an enigma to her, and she didn't like enigmas, she thought defensively. She liked honest, open-faced people like her father had been—and Toby was. She still found it hard to believe that he and Max could be cousins. There couldn't be two men more unalike on this earth.

Her thoughts were still bleak as she let herself into the kitchen, and matters were not improved by finding Max sitting at the table drinking coffee with Aunt Mary.

"So there you are, dear. Just in time for some coffee,"

Aunt Mary said smilingly as Ginny set down her two laden shopping bags on the table with a slight thump.

"I had some in Market Harford, thanks," Ginny said shortly. She looked at Max Hendrick. "Did you want me for something?"

"Not particularly, Ginevra," he said silkily. "I felt in dire need of some female companionship which your great-aunt has charmingly supplied, that's all."

Ginny longed to be able to say something brilliantly sarcastic and probably very rude about his dire needs in relation to women, but as usual nothing occurred to her, so she contented herself with giving him an icy stare before turning her attention to unpacking the shopping.

Aunt Mary continued brightly, "Mr. Hendrick has been telling me all about his home in California, dear. It's quite secluded and almost on the beach itself. Imagine having the Pacific Ocean almost on your doorstep! Doesn't it sound wonderful?"

"I think," Max Hendrick said smoothly, reading her silence with infuriating accuracy, "that Ginny feels it sounds damp. But the climate's wonderful, and I have a driftwood fire on cool evenings."

Ginny did not look at him. "I'm surprised you could bear to leave it and come back to cold, imperfect fog-bound England."

"We have fogs in California too," he said. "And I came back because the lotus-eating life was beginning to have a little too much appeal. I needed to get some serious work done on the new play, and I find England more conducive to work than anywhere else." He paused, then said softly, "And I've let the house in California, so I shan't be returning there for some time to come. Sorry to dash your hopes to the ground, Ginevra."

Ginny lifted her head and encountered the mockery in his glance in silence. It was left to Aunt Mary to murmur deprecatingly that she was quite sure Ginevra was hoping for no such thing, an assurance which Max accepted with one cynically raised eyebrow.

He left soon after that, and as soon as she was certain he was back in his own part of the house and out of earshot, Ginny turned to her great-aunt.

"Aunt Mary, I wish you wouldn't encourage that man to come round here."

"My dear child!" Aunt Mary spoke quellingly. "May I remind you that he is your employer."

"I know that." Ginny held on to her patience. "He pays me to work for him, that's all. He doesn't own me body and soul, and I see quite enough of him in working hours. Every time I turn my back, he seems to be here."

"That," said Aunt Mary with perfect truth, "is a gross exaggeration. I think you're losing your sense of proportion, my child. You must be overtired. I'm sure Mr. Hendrick would allow you to have the afternoon off, if you asked him."

"No," Ginny said grittily. "I don't want any favours from him, nor do I want to give him the impression that I'm some kind of drooping lily who can't face up to a little hard work."

"I'm sure he has the opposite impression. He seems to have the highest opinion of your services, but he did point out that you seemed to have been a little pale over the past couple of days, and did I think he was asking too much of you?"

"There is nothing," Ginny said with dangerous calm, "whatever the matter with me. I know it, and Max Hendrick knows it. The truth is that he probably finds me a disappointment as a secretary, and is looking for an excuse to get rid of me."

"But you're an excellent typist," Aunt Mary protested.

"I think Mr. Hendrick has other rather more exacting requirements of his female employees." Ginny slapped the steak she had bought on to a cutting board, and began to slice it. "If I interested him as a woman, I don't think he'd care what kind of a typist I was."

"My dear!" Aunt Mary's voice was scandalised. "You don't mean that Mr. Hendrick is—has tried...."

"To make a pass at me?" Ginny supplied. "No, of course not. Nor will he. That's what I'm trying to explain. I don't appeal to him in that way, and I expect he wishes now that he'd offered the job to someone who did. Instead, he's stuck with me. In fact we're stuck with each other, because I don't fancy him either," she added defiantly.

"Good heavens," Aunt Mary said rather faintly as Ginny pushed the steak to one side and began fiercely chopping onions and mushrooms.

She had recovered her temper by the time she made her way to the study that afternoon. The knowledge that the casserole was simmering gently in the oven, the grapefruit halved and neatly segmented, and the home-made cheese-cake awaiting the final complement of whipped cream was both calming and satisfying. Cooking, she thought, was decidedly therapeutic, and not even the realisation of who was going to benefit from her preparations could destroy her self-imposed calm. She'd lavished care and attention on the food, pretending to herself that she was cooking it for Toby and herself, and that later that evening it would be the two of them who sat down to eat in the rather faded grandeur of the dining room.

She glanced in at the door on the way to the study and was pleased to see the candlesticks gleaming softly on the table. There was a strong smell of furniture polish in the air, and although Ginny doubted whether the strength of the aroma would have been matched by the amount of elbow-grease expended by Mrs. Petty in applying it, she felt the room would pass muster. In any case, Vivien Lanyon would, she hoped, have eyes only for Max, and not for any forgotten corners or pockets of dust.

She was smiling to herself as she went into the study and was taken aback to find Max sitting on the corner of his desk, clearly impatient.

She said in surprise, "I'm not late, am I?"

"You're a paragon of punctuality," he responded brusquely. "Go and fetch a coat of some kind. We're going out."

Ginny wanted to ask where they were going, and why, but Max's face was so forbidding that her courage failed her, and she went back to get her coat without another word. He was in the hall when she rejoined him, tapping his foot on the polished boards.

"Here." He thrust a notebook and pencil at her, and she crammed them mutely into her pocket, before following him out of the front door and to the car.

A little sigh escaped her as she settled herself in the passenger seat. The last time she had ridden in the car, Toby had been beside her. She was aware that Max had glanced sharply at her and immediately schooled her features to polite impassivity. He seemed to be far too good at reading people's minds, she thought, and there were some thoughts that she preferred to enjoy in private.

He drove well, she had to admit grudgingly. She had expected more aggression and less consideration for others, and suddenly for no reason at all, she remembered a light-hearted article she had read once in a magazine which had suggested that a good way to judge a man's potential as a lover was to watch the way he drove his car. If that was indeed a criterion, then it indicated that Max Hendrick would be very good indeed....

Ginny caught at herself in horror. These were forbidden paths she was treading, she thought, as the colour rose in her face, and heaven help her if Max was doing his thought-reading at this moment. She stole a look at him, and was glad to see his attention appeared to be firmly fixed on the road.

And what road was it? she wondered, as she struggled to regain her composure. She had no idea where they were or how far they had travelled.

When eventually Max pulled the car on to the verge at the side of the road and switched off the engine, she gazed around her in bewilderment. They were in a lane in the middle of gently rolling country, without a house in sight.

"Out you get," he ordered briefly. His door was already open, and after a slight hesitation Ginny climbed out too. It was a fine afternoon, she realised, as she took a deep breath of the sweet air. There seemed to be real strength in the sun for the first time, and only a few lacy clouds disturbed the pale blue of the sky. The branches of the trees still appeared to have the stark bareness of winter, but here and there buds were forming.

Max was beside her, his hand under her arm, urging her forward. They climbed a gate, skirted a field and a small wood and began climbing the broad hump of the hill which lay directly in front of them. She was glad that her shoes had low heels. The track they were using was narrow and rutted and pitted with stones, and she'd be lucky to get to the top without spraining her ankle. If they ever managed to reach the top, she amended breathlessly, wincing from the stitch in her side. Max took her hand and for once she didn't pull away, accepting his help over the last few steep yards.

"Do you mind telling me what we're doing up here?" she demanded when she'd recovered her breath.

"We're admiring the view," he said coolly. "Magnificent, isn't it?"

For a moment words failed her as she stared at him, then she said, "You don't mean you've brought me all the way here just to look at a view?"

"No," he said. "The main purpose of the exercise was to get some colour back into your cheeks, and I'm glad to say in that respect it's been entirely successful."

Speechlessly she tugged the notebook out of her pocket and offered it to him.

"Camouflage," he said mockingly. "If I'd told you we were merely going for a walk, you'd have immediately suspected my motives and refused to come." His smile widened as he watched the dawning comprehension and fury in her eyes, the swift rise and fall of her small breasts. He said, "Why don't you throw it at my head? Then I'd know she was back—that vibrant child who stormed into my kitchen and tried to decapitate me with the crockery. I was afraid she might have been buried for ever under that polite pallid

exterior you seemed determined to present to the world—
or to me at least. As it is, all that's missing at this moment is
the lovelight in your eyes, and I know I couldn't hope to set
that ablaze."

She said unevenly, "You bastard!"

He shrugged lightly. "Call me what you want, Ginevra,
as long as you do it wholeheartedly. Half-people don't appeal to me."

"And in your masculine arrogance," her voice was stony,
"it would never occur to you that I might not want to appeal
to you!"

His mouth twisted slightly. "You've made that more
than clear, but believe it or not it was our working relationship I was seeking to improve—nothing else. Or did you
imagine I'd lured you up here to seduce you? Don't worry,
my sweet, I prefer to take my pleasures in comfort, not
thrashing about in damp undergrowth."

Ginny's face was on fire. She said hotly, "I'm not interested in you, Max Hendrick, or how you conduct your sordid affairs. I don't pretend to know why you brought me
here this afternoon, but I wish you hadn't. Oh, why can't
you leave me alone?" she added bitterly.

"Don't you think that you're alone quite enough as it is?
How old are you—eighteen? You can't be much more, and
yet you've taken on the sort of cares and responsibilities
which would defeat someone twice your age."

"I know what I've taken on, and I chose to do so."

"Very admirable," he said. "But what about you, Ginny? That young, smiling creature I caught a glimpse of
once—where does she fit in among all the cooking and
dusting and typing?"

"I don't think that's any of your business," she said
tonelessly. "As long as I fulfil your requirements in working hours, the rest of my life should be my own. Simply
because we happen to live in the same house it doesn't give
you any proprietorial rights. Now, can we go back, please?
I've still some preparations to make for your dinner party
tonight."

The amusement had faded completely from his face, leaving a bleakness which she endured with lifted chin, her hands buried deep in the pockets of her jacket to conceal the fact that they were trembling.

"You make it very hard for anyone to be your friend," he said at last.

"Not," she said, "if I want their friendship."

Almost as they were uttered, she wished the words unsaid. They were rude and ungracious, and she knew it, but there was something about Max which made her feel raw and vulnerable, which set her constantly on the defensive.

As she followed him down the hill and back to where the car was waiting, she knew, with an instinct more certain than any amount of the experience she lacked, that for her own peace of mind Max Hendrick was a man she needed to keep at more than arm's length.

CHAPTER FOUR

GINNY did not enjoy the drive back to Monk's Dower, but she consoled herself with the fact that nothing else was likely to go wrong on a day which had proved a fair disaster in all sorts of ways.

As the car turned into the courtyard in front of the house, she saw that Tim had returned from school and was desultorily kicking a football around. He came running over to them as the car stopped.

He said, "Aunt Mary was looking for you, Mr. Hendrick. The side piece has come off her glasses, and she was wondering if you could fix it for her."

"I'll certainly have a look," Max promised. He gave Ginny a brief, cold glance as if he was waiting for her to challenge him.

"I tried to mend them," Tim confided, "but Aunt Mary just said I was making things a hundred times worse, and sent me to look for Mouse." He paused. "I looked all over, but I couldn't find either of you, and then we saw the car had gone."

"Mouse?" Max queried, his brows raised.

"That's what we call Ginny—in the family," said Tim, serenely ignoring the anguished look his sister sent him.

Max said coolly, "How singularly inappropriate," and set off for the house. Ginny hung back a little, keeping Tim with her.

"What on earth did you want to tell him that for?" she whispered crossly.

"You mean about your nickname?" Tim stared at her

earnestly. "Because he asked me, of course. What's wrong? Didn't you want him to know?"

"No, I didn't. And it's a silly name anyway."

"Well, I didn't start it." Tim looked very young suddenly, and his lip trembled. "That was Dad's name for you, Ginny."

"Yes, it was." Abashed, she put an arm round his shoulders and gave him a swift hug. "I—I'd forgotten. I'm sorry, Tim. I must be a bit out of sorts today. It's just that— Mr. Hendrick's a stranger, and he's not interested in our private family jokes."

"He is interested in us," Tim insisted. "He often talks to me. He was asking me the other day where we'd lived before—and about school and lots of other things."

Ginny snapped furiously, "Well, I'm damned!" and marched into the house.

The kitchen was deserted, but she could hear voices in the sitting room. Max Hendrick was standing by the window, absorbed in the minute task of repairing the earpiece of her aunt's glasses.

As Ginny came in, with Tim behind her, he said, "I need something to adjust this with. A fine screwdriver—or a nail file would do."

Ginny said reluctantly, "There's one on my dressing table. I'll fetch it for you...."

Tim interposed eagerly, "I'll go. It's all right."

From her armchair, Aunt Mary sighed, "Those wretched glasses! I'm always either losing them or breaking them. I really think I must see about a new pair."

Max smiled at her. When he was not being mocking or cynical, his charm could be quite devastating, Ginny thought sourly, watching him from across the room.

"Why not get one of those elegant chains as well, so that you can hang them round your neck?" he suggested. "My grandmother had one. She used to call it the blessing of the absentminded."

Aunt Mary, Ginny thought with satisfaction, would not relish being numbered among the absentminded, even by implication, and she waited expectantly for a ladylike but icy blast to sweep Max Hendrick from the face of the earth.

But her great-aunt was returning his smile, and murmuring something about "an excellent notion." Oh, well done, Mr. Clever Hendrick, Ginny said in seething silence. Everyone's favourite but mine.

Tim came hurtling down the stairs. "I've got the nail file," he announced. "And I found this as well, Ginny. It's a picture of Barbie, isn't it? Where did you get it from?"

She could have groaned aloud as she saw the leather folder clutched in his hand. It was too late to tell him starkly to put it back where he found it and not meddle, because Aunt Mary had pricked up her ears and was holding out her hand.

"A picture of dear Barbara? How very thoughtful of her to send it, particularly when we see so little of her these days."

"You'll see a lot more of her now," Ginny thought miserably as Aunt Mary opened the folder and accepted the mended glasses from Max Hendrick with a word of thanks. Her expression did not change as she looked at the photograph, but Ginny saw her great-aunt's back stiffen almost imperceptibly.

Tim said irrepressibly, "She looks gorgeous, doesn't she? You wouldn't think she and Ginny were sisters, would you, Max?"

Standing beside Miss Clayton's chair, Max Hendrick looked down at the picture. Ginny felt a tight knot of tension tie itself within her, as if a great deal depended on his reaction and not just because of Tim's tactless remark. Her eyes were fixed on his face, and only she saw the odd expression which crossed it momentarily—shock blended with recognition, she would have sworn, and her heart sank within her like a stone.

"No," he said coolly after a moment, and his eyes met hers, enigmatic and guarded. "There's barely any resemblance."

As she turned away, Ginny supposed rather bitterly that

she could have expected nothing better from him. Not that she wanted it, she hastened to assure herself. His admiration was as unwanted as his good opinion. At least, she amended, she wanted him to acknowledge that she was a good secretary. She wanted him to have no complaints about her professional standards, at all.

By the time she had been upstairs to take her jacket off, he had gone back to his own part of the house, and she was thankful as she cast a critical but satisfied eye over her arrangements for the meal.

At the same time, she couldn't help wondering where Max Hendrick had met Barbara, because her sister had been adamant that he was unknown to her. Wasn't that why she had sent the photograph in the first place—to engage his attention? Unless, Ginny thought unhappily, it was to stir his memory. Perhaps Barbie had simply not wanted to admit to her younger sister that she and her employer had once been only too well acquainted.

She put down the vegetable knife she was using, feeling a little sick. It had often seemed to her that the entire theatrical profession was one of pretence. If Max and her sister were fair examples of its membership, then all her assumptions were fully justified, she thought bitterly. Max hadn't betrayed the slightest glimmer of recognition when she had mentioned Barbie's name to him when they had first met. And yet her face had been instantly familiar to him. Ginny thought that she did not want to consider the implications of that at all.

She tried to put the whole unpleasant little incident out of her mind, but it wasn't easy, and she was unusually snappish over tea with Tim and Aunt Mary. The latter remarking acidly that her outing did not seem to have improved her temper.

She felt more at peace with herself when she had completed the laying of the dining table a few hours later. The polished surface reflected back the silver and glassware, and the bowl of early spring flowers she had arranged as a centrepiece. She stood back to admire it, deciding at the same time to leave the lighting of the candles until the last minute.

Max's voice said just behind her, "Very elegant."

Ginny whirled round, her heart thumping painfully. "I didn't hear you come in. I—I was just making sure that everything was ready."

"Everything looks fine," he said. He was frowning a little. "It's been a great deal of work for you. I'm sorry. Next time I plan anything like this, I'll make other arrangements."

"If you're not satisfied—" she began stiffly, but his interruption was swift and sharp.

"I'm perfectly satisfied, you prickly little monster! Haven't I made that clear? Believe it or not, I'm concerned about you. Obviously I haven't made that clear enough either."

"I don't want your concern." She lifted her chin and stared at him resentfully. She had to admit his attraction. Tonight it was almost overwhelming. He was an elegant stranger in narrow-legged dark slacks, a velvet jacket and a silk shirt open at the throat. The lean gipsy in the faded denims and rollneck sweater had vanished completely, and she was at a loss now to deal with the Max Hendrick who had taken his place. But she was suddenly, inexplicably glad that she did not have to. That it was Vivien Lanyon and not herself who was to be overwhelmed and won.

Max raised his eyebrows. "Have I suddenly grown another head?"

Ginny flushed, realising that she had been staring at him, and hoped her face had not betrayed her inner thoughts.

"I was just wondering whether I'd forgotten something," she said rather stiltedly.

"I wouldn't have thought so," he said rather impatiently. "For God's sake, Ginny, relax! Whenever I'm around, you behave as if you're strung up on wires. Why? Are you afraid that I'll make a pass at you?"

"Such an eventuality never even occurred to me," she said, aware of an odd constriction in her throat. "I think your past conquests must have gone to your head."

There was an electrifying pause, and then he said too smoothly, "Of course, that must be it. How very perceptive of you, Ginevra. Are you equally adept, I wonder, at examining your own motivations and responses?"

He took one long step forward. She tried to back away, but the heavy length of the dining table was behind her, preventing all but the most token retreat. She leaned back against it, feeling the smooth polished edge bite into the palms of her hands, while Max loomed above her like some dark, inexorable bird of prey, and she swallowed convulsively, closing her eyes and her mind against the anger and more than anger that she sensed in him.

His hands were gripping her arms, bruising her, and she gasped with the pain, but more than the pain as he drew her against him, and her senses absorbed the warmth of him, the uncompromising hardness of bone and muscle beneath the silk and velvet, the unique scent of his skin intermingled with the expensive sharpness of some cologne he used.

The darkness was roaring behind her tightly pressed eyelids, lit up with tiny golden sparks, and the same sparks were flaring deep within her, igniting a flame undiscovered and unsuspected that threatened to consume her utterly.

She could not see, or speak or hear, she could only feel, and sensation exploded around her and inside her, and his mouth on hers was the world's sweetest agony. The golden light behind her eyelids, and the golden flame within her were one, and she could taste blood on her lips because he had not been gentle.

And somewhere in her consciousness, there was a noise, shocking in its intrusion, and even as she registered it, Max's hands left her and she felt him move away. The flame died and the darkness poured back, and she opened dazed eyes and looked at him.

He said coolly, "I think that's what's known as being saved by the bell. My visitor seems to have arrived."

For a moment or two his words would not penetrate, and she went on staring at him, then, as she realised what he had said, a shiver went through her, and she lifted an incredulous hand to her bruised and trembling mouth.

He said with a trace of impatience, "Don't look so shattered, Ginevra. It was only a kiss, after all. Perhaps it will teach you not to provoke me into losing my temper in future."

He turned and went out of the room as the door bell shrilled again imperatively. Engulfed in shame, Ginny ran to the kitchen, slamming the door and leaning against the elderly panels for a moment while she regained her breath and her tottering equilibrium.

How could I? she thought wildly. How could I have let him kiss me like that?

She wanted to run, to put a million miles between them, so that she would never have to face him again, and instead she had to take the grapefruit through and place it on the table, set the vegetables to simmer on the stove and check the seasoning in her casserole—arrange all the last details for the dinner which presently she would serve. And she couldn't even yield to her insane, childish urge to sweep all her careful preparations into one glutinous mess on the floor because there were Tim and Aunt Mary to think about. In spite of everything that had happened, she needed this job, she needed the money and the security of this roof over their heads. She had created this trap and now it had closed behind her.

She shivered, putting her hands over her face. She had been so sure she would be able to cope, that somehow she would make this new life work for them all. Now she felt very young and afraid and alone. The mature and responsible image of herself she had struggled so hard to foster lay shattered in a thousand fragments.

Oh, it was so easy for Max Hendrick and all the other predators of this world, she thought furiously. They stalked through life, taking what they wanted with both hands, leaving their victims looted and bleeding behind them.

The thought reminded her of something else. Tentatively she passed her tongue across her lips, then went over to her handbag and found a small mirror. Her mouth looked

slightly swollen, but that was all, and in the dim lighting of
the dining room she hoped she would pass muster. The last
thing she wanted to happen was for Vivien Lanyon to suspect that Max had been making love to her. Ginny knew
that if one word of what had just transpired reached Mrs.
Lanyon's ears, then her days at Monk's Dower would be
numbered.

Angrily she raked her dishevelled hair into obedience
with her fingers, and disguised the blurred contours of her
mouth with lipstick. Then she picked up the bowls of grapefruit and carried them towards the door. It opened abruptly
as she reached it, almost knocking the tray from her hands,
and she froze as Max came in.

He said sharply and without preamble, "Are you all
right?"

"Of course I am." Her tone matched his, except for a
slight breathlessness she strove hard to disguise. "What did
you think—that I'd be having a fit of the vapours like a
Victorian parlourmaid?"

"Hardly." He paused. "If it makes any difference, I'm
prepared to apologise."

"That's big of you," she said. "But you really don't have
to. I'm not a child any more—and I take your point about
not provoking you."

He said slowly, "Ginny, I know what you must be thinking and...."

"I'm not thinking anything," she said in a rather high
voice. "I promise you I'm not. And aren't you keeping
your guest waiting? Perhaps you'd let me know when
you're ready to eat."

"The Victorian parlourmaid rears her ugly head," he said
jeeringly. "Where's your cap and apron, Ginny?"

"I daresay I could find one to wear," she said. "And I'd
wear it too if that's what is needed to remind you that I'm
your servant in many ways. It's not a thought I relish particularly, and you don't make it any easier for me." She
swallowed. "Now will you let me pass, please? I have work
to do."

"Then you'd better get on with it," he said grimly. "But you and I are due for a talk about your exact status here."

"I have no status here, so there's nothing to discuss." Ginny felt profoundly weary and oddly close to tears. "I can accept that, Mr. Hendrick, so why can't you? I'll do the work which I'm paid for, and all I want in return is to be left alone. It's that simple."

Simple, something within her mocked, when at any moment you'll remember what it was like to be in his arms—the touch of his mouth? Simple?

She heard herself say in a voice like a stone, "Unless of course you feel that the fact that I'm Barbie Nicholas's sister gives you some kind of rights. It doesn't, actually. You said yourself only today that we weren't at all alike. Perhaps you should remember that."

"Perhaps I should," Max agreed. He hadn't moved a muscle, but she had the curious sensation that the million miles she had longed for was now between them, and she felt the chill of isolation. He turned away and went out of the kitchen and she had an impulse to go after him and tell him that she hadn't meant to say that, that the truth of his relationship with Barbie had been nagging at her ever since she had watched him look at her sister's photograph, and that some inner demon had put those words into her mouth.

But she couldn't do that because any such admission on her part would almost sound as if she was jealous, and she wasn't—she wasn't, she told herself fiercely. Any slight pangs she might have suffered were not on Max Hendrick's behalf but on Barbie's, because it seemed as if some of the suspicions she had harboured about the way her sister led her life might be true.

Yet even that is none of my concern, she thought, as she walked down the passage to the dining room, and set the grapefruit down in their appointed places. Barbie's a grown woman and she can look after herself. She lit the tall red candles and left the room, just as Mrs. Lanyon came out of the drawing room opposite with Max just behind her.

"Good heavens!" The older woman's eyes swept Ginny from head to foot. "Of course, I'd almost forgotten I'd hired this child for you, Max. Is she proving satisfactory? Don't tell me you trusted her with the dinner tonight? If you'd only told me you were stuck for someone to do the cooking, I'd have sent you my Mrs. Marsh."

"I'm sure Ginny has managed perfectly well," he said colourlessly. "She's very efficient in every way, thank you."

"Good." Vivien Lanyon laid a hand on his arm, smiling up at him. She wore a full-length tapestry skirt in muted shades of green, gold and bronze, and a black silk jersey top which moulded itself closely to her figure, accentuating the voluptuous fullness of her breasts. As she brushed past Ginny, she could smell the musky fragrance of the scent she wore. There was little sign tonight of the regal lady of the manor. Vivien Lanyon was just a beautiful sensual woman making little secret of her attraction to the tall man beside her. It was difficult to decide, Ginny thought detachedly, who was stalking whom, or who would emerge as the eventual victor. As predators, they seemed well matched.

She was glad that she hadn't yielded to the temptation to tip half a packet of salt into the casserole. It looked and smelled delicious as she lifted it out of the oven where it had completed its cooking. Next time, she thought, she would risk cooking the whole meal from start to finish in the wood stove—then remembered that Max had said there wouldn't be a next time. She ladled the broccoli spears and baby carrots into their serving dishes, and took the foil from the jacket potatoes. Then she loaded everything on to a tray and carried it carefully along to the dining room.

They had finished their grapefruit and were ready for the next course, but all the same she felt that her arrival was an unwanted intrusion. As she set the dishes down, she was aware that Vivien Lanyon was watching her with narrowed eyes, and her intuition told her that the other woman was hoping that the meal would be a disaster.

Social conventions made life very difficult, she thought

ruefully as she went back to the kitchen and began to make
herself a cup of coffee. It would be much easier if she could
turn to Vivien Lanyon and say, "You have nothing to fear
from me. I made him angry, that was all, and he thought of
an ideal way to punish me. But it will never happen again,
I'll see to that." She shook her head slightly as she filled the
kettle and set it on the stove to boil, before beginning to
assemble the filter and jug to make the coffee for the drawing room. The brandy and liqueurs were already in there,
she knew, in one of the tall cupboards which stood in the
alcoves beside the fireplace.

When she had drunk her coffee, she went along to the
drawing room and made up the fire. Then on an impulse
she switched off the main light, leaving one tall standard
lamp and a smaller one on a table near the window as the
only means of illumination. At once the room seemed
smaller and more intimate. She moved over to the sofa and
plumped up the cushions which had become disarranged,
then collected the used sherry glasses and took them back
to the kitchen.

The cheesecake she had already placed on the dining
room sideboard, so that they could serve themselves when
they were ready. All she had left to do was take the coffee
tray along to the drawing room, and wash up. Then she
could go back to her own part of the house and relax.

She was watching the last of the coffee filter through into
the jug when Max came in. Her thoughts had been a long
way away, and she jumped almost guiltily when she heard
the sound of his voice.

He said, "That was a superb meal, Ginny. I'm more than
grateful. If the coffee's ready, I'll take it through, and you
can go home."

"But the washing up—" she began.

"I can manage a few dishes." His voice was dismissive.
"You've had a long day, so run along now, like a good girl."

She was about to protest that she could at least clear the
table when she suddenly realised that she was being got rid
of. She had served her purpose and now she could go, and

leave him and his guest in privacy. A dull flush stole into her cheeks.

"Thank you." She knew she sounded lame. "If—if you want to leave the dishes until the morning . . . ."

"I've told you I can manage." There was more than a tinge of impatience in his tone. "Besides, the weekend is your own. I want that clearly understood."

And he also wanted her to understand that when morning came he might not be alone, and her arrival would only be an embarrassment, she realised bleakly. She set the jug of coffee on the tray and handed it to him mutely.

He said, "So that's settled, is it? You don't appear here again until Monday morning."

She said in a low voice, "You've made it all perfectly clear, Mr. Hendrick."

She stood and stared at the floor until she knew she was alone, then walked across to the kitchen table to get her bag. She gave a groan of dismay as she picked it up and realised that it was masking the sugar basin. Max didn't take sugar in his coffee, but Vivien Lanyon probably did, and she didn't want even the slightest black mark against her.

The drawing room door was ajar, and as she touched the handle it swung silently inwards before she could knock.

It was almost as if she was watching a play. They were standing on the hearthrug in front of the fire, locked in each other's arms. Vivien Lanyon's body was thrusting against his without reticence, her arms twining round his neck as if she was endeavouring to draw him even closer.

For a few seconds, Ginny stood there as if she had been turned to stone, then she turned and crept noiselessly away. She returned the unwanted sugar to the kitchen and sped back to her own part of the house, her heart beating abnormally fast as she let herself in.

She was thankful that neither of them had turned and seen her, standing there as if she had been transfixed. And yet what else should she have expected? It had been made more than clear to her that she was in the way, and she herself had provided the romantic setting—the warmth, the dim lighting, the inviting sofa. She hadn't expected the love scene to start so soon, that was all. Nor was it the sort of tentative embrace that strangers might be expected to exchange, but she'd had no reason to expect that either. Kathy had warned her after all. Perhaps the affair had begun even before Max officially moved into Monk's Dower—even while the negotiations over the tenancy were taking place, she thought, with a feeling of distaste.

Yet what right had she to react in any way, when all was said and done? If she'd ever had any illusions about Max's proclivities, his treatment of herself would have destroyed them. He was a womaniser of the most contemptible kind, she thought stormily, and the realisation of that made her unthinking, involuntary response to him even more shameful.

She could only be thankful that Vivien Lanyon had arrived when she did and prevented her from making an even bigger fool of herself.

Pleading tiredness, she went to bed early, but she could not sleep. She tossed and turned from side to side, seeking a cool place on the pillow, trying desperately to settle, while with a part of her mind she did not even wish to acknowledge she listened in vain for the sound of Vivien Lanyon's departure.

In the early hours of the morning, she thought, "Air. I must have some air," and she got out of bed and padded across to the window, to open one of the casements. It was a clear night, the sky bright with stars, and she shivered a little as the shaft of frosty air hit her thinly clad body.

Despising herself, she glanced down towards the front door of the house. Monk's Dower seemed to be in total darkness, but she could make out the unmistakable shape of a second car parked beside Max's. For a long moment she stood looking at it. Well, she thought, so now she knew. So her curiosity was satisfied. They were still together.

She let the curtain fall back into place and crept back to bed, where she lay chilled, confused and more miserable, she realised with utter dismay, than she had any right to be.

GINNY spent the weekend in a positive orgy of cleaning and baking, until their part of the house gleamed and every cake tin was full. Aunt Mary and Tim watched her with faint astonishment, but neither of them cared to question her activities. There was a kind of frenetic energy about her which did not invite speculation.

Both cars had vanished from the courtyard quite early on Saturday morning, as she hadn't been able to help noticing, but she refused to allow herself to consider the implications of what had happened any further. After all, she thought, she had never had any illusions about Max Hendrick. In fact, all that recent events had done was reinforce her first impressions of him.

Muffin escaped again on Sunday afternoon and Ginny realised guiltily, after he had returned home and been scolded, that she had completely forgotten to hand on Kathy's warning to Tim. As she had half expected, he received it indignantly.

"Muffin wouldn't hurt anything," he expostulated. "He's a friendly dog. If he did chase an animal, it would only be because he wanted to play."

As gently as possible Ginny explained that his victim might not understand this, and that the dividing line between playing and worrying was a very thin one.

"Well, sheep and chickens must be utterly brainless, then," Tim muttered, and took himself off to his bedroom, ostensibly to do his homework, but really, Ginny suspected, to read lurid war comics in privacy. She suppressed a sigh. Tim was beginning to prove something of a handful. Perhaps a not-very-much-older sister and an elderly great-aunt were not the ideal people to cope with a lively boy, and that social worker had had a point after all. She caught herself up in alarm. That was defeatist talk, and it was also untrue. It was just that life seemed rather bleak and depressing at the moment, that was all. She could cope, of course she could.

She was tight-lipped and unsmiling when she reported for work on Monday morning, and discovered somewhat to her surprise that Max was in much the same humour. There was a suitcase standing in the hall, and when she went into the study she found Max flinging papers into a briefcase and swearing under his breath.

"I have to go to London for a few days," he said briefly. "You can complete the revisions on Act One and start the first draft of Act Two. That should keep you occupied."

"Oh." Ginny, who had nerved herself for this meeting, was nonplussed. "Will you be away long? Are there problems?"

Max shrugged. "Of course there are problems, or I wouldn't be going. I'm hoping to sort them out before they become mountains instead of molehills, but how long it will take is one of the great imponderables. Your guess is as good as mine. Do you have a vital reason for asking?"

"It's just that—I have to know what to tell people—callers."

He sent her a sardonic glance. "Most of my potential callers will already know where I am. Any others—tell them what you know and no more. Fair enough?"

"I suppose so," she muttered, wondering which category Vivien Lanyon would be found in.

"What's the matter?" Max fastened his briefcase, his eyes challenging as they met hers. "You look positively dejected. I thought the prospect of a few days without me would be a boost for your morale."

"It's really none of my business where you go or what you do," she waid woodenly, her mind reverting in spite of herself to the events of the weekend.

"Oh, but it is, while you continue to act as my secretary. I don't expect you to cry into your pillow, but I do expect you to take an intelligent interest. After all—"he was still watching her"—one of these days, I might expect you to come with me."

"Oh." She was really startled. "But I couldn't."

"Why not? The others did."

"Yes, well, perhaps so," she said totally at a loss. "But they were different."

His eyes narrowed. "You think so? Perhaps one day we might profitably discuss your view of the exact nature of that difference, but I haven't time now." At the door he flung her a glance, half considering, half mocking. "Besides," he remarked almost casually, "on the evidence so far, perhaps you aren't as different as you like to think."

Ginny stood glaring helplessly at the door he had closed behind him, her face burning. She knew exactly what he meant. Oh, why had she allowed him to kiss her, or why hadn't she at least slapped his face or kicked his shins or done something to indicate that she wanted no involvement with him in that way? By her silence she had allowed him to draw his own humiliating conclusions.

Damn him, she thought, her hands curling into impotent balls of fury at her sides. Why didn't he stay in London so that she never had to see him again?

Loss of temper had an adverse effect on her typing, and after about three-quarters of an hour, she gave it up as a bad job, and went along to the kitchen to make some coffee for herself and for Mrs. Petty who was unenthusiastically pushing a Hoover about to the accompaniment of a sentimental ballad, sung loudly and untunefully.

Ginny was on her way back to the study when the front door opened abruptly and Vivien Lanyon came in, her arms full of flowers.

"What are you doing here?" was her immediate, ungracious question.

Ginny gulped, annoyed that her instinctive start of surprise had caused her to splash coffee on the usually immaculate boards.

"Working," she said, with a quick, nervous gesture towards the study.

Mrs. Lanyon's eyes narrowed. "Surely you should have finished by now. There's no need for you to remain in this part of the house while Mrs. Petty is working. A quick check just before she leaves is all that's necessary."

Ginny said, "I mean my other work—the typing."

"Typing?" The older woman's brows arched in amazement. "Since when have you been typing for Mr. Hendrick?"

"Ever since he arrived," Ginny admitted.

"I see." There was a brief silence, then Vivien Lanyon said thinly, "You're clearly a girl of many talents. The meal on Friday was quite impressive. And now you type as well— I don't remember you mentioning that at our initial meeting. I might have had an opening for you in the estate office. My present girl is often rushed off her feet. I'd have thought as I was prepared to provide you with a roof over your head, I might have received prior consideration."

Ginny said tautly, "I didn't intend to become anyone's secretary. Mr. Hendrick discovered I could type quite by accident. I hadn't planned to be anything more than the housekeeper."

"Very wise," said Vivien Lanyon, and smiled. "But whatever you may have planned, my dear, you seem to have—wormed your way in here quite successfully. I hope you won't let it go to your head. Now—" she thrust the flowers she was holding towards Ginny, "go and find me some vases for these. The place could do with brightening up. I thought so the other evening."

Ginny's hands were shaking as she put her coffee mug down and went back to the kitchen. But in spite of a prolonged search, none of the containers she was able to produce satisfied Mrs. Lanyon's exacting standards.

"You really have no idea at all, do you?" she sighed irritably, waving away the vases and jugs assembled for her inspection on the kitchen table. "I suppose I'll have to find something at the Manor. It's just as well this job is just a temporary measure for you. You wouldn't last five minutes with a really exacting employer."

She meant, with a woman living at Monk's Dower, Ginny thought, after Mrs. Lanyon had gone. Someone with an eagle eye for Mrs. Petty's shortcomings, who would expect flowers and ornaments to be arranged with verve and flair. Perhaps she even meant herself. Ginny didn't know. All she knew was that the words "temporary measure" had struck a chill through her. She had hoped this refuge at Monk's Dower was hers for the foreseeable future.

And it might have been as well, she knew instinctively, only Vivien Lanyon had decided against her. From now on Mrs. Lanyon would be looking for an excuse to be rid of her, because she was young and female and spent too much time with Max Hendrick.

Ginny thought, "How unsure she must be of him—and of herself." And a feeling almost of pity penetrated the cloud of sick despair which was beginning to envelop her.

She gave a little groan. Where could they go? What could they do, when the chop finally came as she was sure now it would? The prospect was murder, and in some twisted way it was all Max's fault. If he'd been less desirable, she found herself thinking, then this situation would never have arisen.

Desirable? The colour rose in her face. What a word to use, and about a man! It had never entered her vocabulary before. She'd had the usual crushes on pop stars and actors as a young girl, but more because it was fashionable, and she would have been an oddity among her school contemporaries if she had not joined in, than through any real conviction.

She'd been wary too of the trap she'd seen some of her friends fall into—a single-minded devotion to someone barely older than themselves, followed by early marriage as soon as they left school. She hadn't wanted that, any more than she had wanted the kind of casual promiscuity that some of the others went in for, so she had stayed aloof.

She'd been able to say, "I fancy So-and-so," but always with a laugh, never with any underlying seriousness. And it had never been more than fancy either—a fleeting whimsical preference, not strong enough to withstand the cold light of day and common sense.

But desire was different. That was serious, that was heavy. She tried to tell herself that it must be her almost total lack of any previous experience which made her remember Max's kiss in such minute and intimate detail that her body began to tremble, but the excuse didn't sound convincing, even to herself.

She thought in panic, "Oh God, what's happening to me? I don't want to remember that. I don't need that. I need to think—to plan—to decide what to do when the worst happens."

Her coffee was cold and bitter now, and she tipped it away with a grimace. She ought to go back to the study and start again on the work Max had left, but she knew she would be unable to concentrate properly, and not just because she was worried about the future. It was the recent past which filled her thoughts so ominously, and there were implications in that which she did not even want to consider.

As she walked to the door, her eyes went to the splash of colour in the sink, where Vivien Lanyon's flowers survived, up to their pretty necks in a bucket of cold water.

She said aloud and defiantly, "And I'll survive too." Then she walked out of the kitchen and slammed the door behind her.

CHAPTER FIVE

MAX was gone for over a week, and Vivien Lanyon's charmingly elaborate flower arrangements passed their best and had to be discarded. She continued to make her presence felt, however, and Ginny began to feel hunted as the days went by. There was hardly a day when Vivien Lanyon did not call or telephone, and even Mrs. Petty began to grumble at the new régime.

"If Madam isn't satisfied with the way things are, then she'll have to find someone else, or I'll have to come in more days," she declared truculently to Ginny, hands on hips. "It's a big house to keep up—especially the way she wants it."

Ginny murmured that she was sure Mrs. Lanyon was perfectly satisfied really, but it was untrue. In fact Vivien Lanyon seemed obsessed with asserting her authority, and re-establishing the fact that although Max Hendrick might be living in Monk's Dower, she was the owner, and had the last word.

Perhaps, Ginny thought wryly, she was also establishing that she owned Max Hendrick. Well, she told herself with a touch of defiance, they were more than welcome to each other, both arrogant and unlikeable.

She managed at last to get Max's work finished, and she left the completed sheets, together with the rough draft and his notes in the study. She felt curiously restive once it was finished, although really she should have welcomed the freedom it brought her. The weather seemed to be getting warmer every day, and this was the perfect opportunity to explore the surrounding countryside, the hills and soft rolling meadows, the trees and hedges just coming into blossom and leaf. The beauty of the slowly gathering spring seemed to call out to her, but Ginny herself resisted its imperious summons with something like panic.

What point was there in discovering her surroundings, in learning to love and appreciate them, when she might not be here for very much longer? There was so much she could enjoy, so much to catch at her heart, and she just could not allow it to happen. Becoming attached to places, to people, would only make her vulnerable. She could not even encourage her own secret pleasure in the fact that Monk's Dower, even without the addition of flower arrangements, was beginning to lose its lonely and neglected atmosphere, and take on the lived-in, cared-for ambience of a real home. Only it wasn't her real home, and she must never permit herself to forget that. It was a temporary measure. She had to keep remembering that. It had been a word of warning from Vivien Lanyon that she would ignore at her peril.

She would have liked desperately to confide in Aunt Mary, but her great-aunt had a slight cold, and was not too well, and Ginny had no desire to give her any additional worry. And Tim was nowhere near an age to be a recipient of confidences. There was no one she could talk to, she thought miserably. Even if she ran into Kathy again and told her of her worries, she was pretty sure the older woman would only remind her that she had told her so.

Almost fatalistically, she turned her back on the glimmer of sunshine, moving restlessly from room to room, admiring their old-fashioned spaciousness, their settled air, even the patina on the furniture. She liked old houses. She'd been brought up in one, after all, though it wasn't nearly as old as Monk's Dower.

She chose books at random from the glass-fronted cupboards in the study and the rarely used morning room, but even though reading was one of her passions, and one that she had had little time to indulge in recent months, few of her choices were able to hold her interest for very long.

Sometimes as she wandered round, she found herself imagining what it would be like to own a house like Monk's Dower, to live in it and know it as home. She thought she would like it, found herself planning new colour schemes, replacing faded chintzes and brocades. She could imagine children, too, playing hide and seek in the upstairs passages. A house needed children, especially one that had been used for generations for a succession of elderly dowagers.

But the face of the potential master of the house—the man who would supply the money for the refurbishment, and provide the children—remained shadowy, however determinedly she tried to visualise him. It was Toby's face she always tried to call to mind, naturally, yet it did not seem quite to fit—like a wrong piece in a jigsaw. Except that this time it was the wrong jigsaw as well, she thought with a stifled sigh.

Her idiotic fancies were running away with her, but it was so much easier to indulge them than to face reality. All the same, she knew that Monk's Dower would never be hers. It had been in the Lanyon family for centuries. Vivien Lanyon would never let it go. She would never let anything go that belonged to her. Ginny remembered her hand on Max Hendrick's sleeve, the manicured fingers curling possessively. Remembered her arms twining round his neck, drawing him down to her.

Ginny felt a shudder run through her, and she recoiled from the picture she had deliberately evoked. It was an image she had tried to banish from her mind, in the same way as she had avoided going into Max's bedroom. She'd asked Mrs. Petty to clean the room and change the sheets on the wide bed, so that she would not have to, and she trusted to luck that her instructions had been properly carried out, because wild horses were not going to drag her in there to look.

She was being both foolish and prudish, she knew, but she couldn't help it. It was the way she was. She was the last person in the world to be involved with a man who conducted his private life as flagrantly as Max Hendrick seemed to do.

The most disturbing thing she had to remember was the way he had held her in his arms and kissed her, only seconds before he answered the door to his mistress. Ginny thought she would never forgive him for that. Perhaps she hadn't been able to conceal her agitation, her blatantly ruffled feathers sufficiently well to fool Vivien Lanyon, and that was why her days at Monk's Dower seemed to be numbered.

Or perhaps, and even less bearable to contemplate, he had made a joking confession—"Darling, I actually made a pass at the hired help." Vivien Lanyon would have laughed with him—too clever to betray jealousy or malice openly—but later....

Ginny shook her head. These were fantasy realms again. Max had kissed her because he had been momentarily provoked into irritation. It was unlikely in the extreme that he had mentioned it to anyone, or even given it a second thought himself since. It was she herself who was making a trivial incident into a big deal. But why? The only answer that suggested itself was that she was lonely, and that any incident in her staid existence was likely to assume undue importance.

She gave a slight grimace. Dull and prim—like the Victorian parlourmaid she had denied being. But even Victorian parlourmaids enjoyed themselves sometimes, she thought. Even if they were officially forbidden "followers," they must have managed to introduce a little excitement into their humdrum lives. Whereas she, a child of the sixties and seventies, spent her days like a novice nun.

She turned away from the window out of which she had been gazing quite unseeingly at a bed of daffodils, and nearly stumbled over Muffin who had followed her from their own part of the house as he sometimes did.

"Oh, Muff!" She bent to fondle his ears penitently. "You really shouldn't be here, you know."

Although no longer a puppy he still had his rumbustious moments, occasionally forgetting his manners sufficiently to chew up slippers and other items which lay in his path.

He was, Ginny had always suspected, a dog with a low boredom threshold. Perhaps this was why he made his now infrequent dashes for freedom. Tim had recoverd from his fit of sulks and was meticulous about keeping Muffin on a lead during their walks, so that was one worry less for Ginny.

She took hold of his collar to urge him back to their own wing when she heard the sound of the car engine, and stiffened instantly. It wasn't Max's car, she saw as she straightened and stared through the window again. It was a smaller vehicle, one of those produced for the mass market.

Muffin hurled himself in the direction of the front door barking hysterically, and at that moment a familiar figure got out of the driving seat, and came towards the house.

Ginny thought on a rising surge of joy. Toby? No, it can't be.

Only a few minutes earlier she had been playing her game of trying to build the image of him in her mind, and now here he was, as if she had conjured him like a genie from a lamp.

She flew to the door in Muffin's wake, and tore it open. The dog shot out ahead of her, whining and leaping up and down at Toby, who leaned down laughingly to pat him. He was still smiling as he looked at Ginny.

"Hello, love. Missed me?"

She wanted to tell him how much, but she was suddenly tongue-tied. All she could say was, "You didn't tell us you were coming. I haven't got a room ready for you."

He shrugged. "It was a last-minute decision. And you don't have to bother about a room. I'm not staying here. I've booked in at the White Hart in Market Harford."

There was no way she could hide her disappointment as she stared at him. "The White Hart? But why?"

"Cousin Max's orders. It was made very clear to me that he doesn't need any house guests. Well—" he grinned deprecatingly "—he doesn't need me, anyway. I've been warned off."

"But why should he do such a thing?" she demanded hotly. "It's the meanest thing I've ever heard!"

Toby shrugged again. "Max is an enigma, and always has

been," he said. "He was kind enough to me when I was a child, I suppose, but in recent years relations between us could best be described as strained. In spite of that, could we bend the rules sufficiently for me to have a cup of coffee, do you think?" He grimaced. "That brew they serve at the White Hart should be sued under the Trades Description Act!"

She started. "Of course. I—I didn't mean to keep you on the doorstep. Come in."

He walked past her, snapping his fingers for Muffin to follow him.

"It's good to see you, Ginny," he said, slipping off the leather car coat he was wearing. "And how's Tim, and that amazing aunt of yours?"

"We're all fine," she answered shyly. Seeing Toby again, having him so close, was like waking from a dream to find it had come true, and she wasn't sure she could cope with that kind of happiness.

"You look wonderful." He followed her to the kitchen and stood watching while she put on the kettle. "Is country life agreeing with you, or is it the heady adventure of working for Cousin Max?"

"Well, it certainly isn't that," she said tartly.

He laughed, but his eyes were searching. "Don't tell me that for once Max has come across a female resistant to his charm. I can hardly believe it."

She measured coffee into the beakers. "Perhaps he doesn't bother to use his charm where I'm concerned. I only work for him, after all." She hesitated. "Did you know I was his secretary as well?"

"I think it was mentioned," he said casually. "Well, perhaps Max has learned his lesson. Usually his secretaries go down like ninepins before him, and start boring him to death with their undying devotion."

"Well, he needn't worry about that with me," Ginny snapped. She shifted the beakers on the worktop, then said slowly, "Toby, why did you let me think that you'd rented the house—that I would be working for you?"

He looked slightly abashed. "I haven't really got a good reason, or one that makes any sense." He sighed. "I suppose I just enjoyed playing master of the house for a time. You see, Ginny, our family has always been divided into two factions—the haves and the have-nots, and Max's side is very definitely the former. Apart from the fortune he makes from his plays, his parents left him comfortably off. All the black sheep in the family are on our side of the fence. My father was always a bit of a gambler, and Uncle Richard—that's Max's father—had to bail us out quite a few times. So, when I got the chance to step into his shoes for a few weeks, I took it." He grinned ruefully. "I'm afraid his lordship was not pleased about it, hence my banishment to the White Hart. Oh, by the way—"he produced an envelope, addressed to her in Max's distinctive angular script and handed it over"—I have this to deliver."

Ginny accepted it in surprise, and tore the envelope open. It contained a note and a cheque for an amount which made her blink. For a dazed moment she wondered if Max was paying her in lieu of notice, and her hand shook as she unfolded the note.

Its contents were brief and to the point. He was still having problems, he wrote, and couldn't say definitely when he would be back. However, he was enclosing her wages, together with a small extra sum for doing the cooking for him—his idea of small, Ginny thought peevishly—and he was hers, Max. As an afterthought he included a telephone number where he could be reached in case of emergency.

"What's the matter?" Toby asked.

She swallowed. "Nothing, I suppose. It's just this." She held the cheque out and he glanced at it with raised brows.

"What's wrong with it? It's dated, signed, everything in order, isn't it?"

"Yes, but that's not the point. It's far too much. Much more than we agreed."

Toby gave her an amazed look. "Does it matter, sweetheart? Max can afford it, I promise you. Take it and be thankful."

"But I don't feel I've earned it," she protested.

"Well, no doubt he intends that you will in future," Toby said rather drily. "The kettle's boiling, in case you hadn't noticed."

"What? Oh." She swooped on it, and poured hot water on to the coffee granules. "What do you mean?"

"Not a great deal," he said unconvincingly. "Forget it."

"I don't think I can." She stirred the coffee slowly. "You mean it's in the nature of a bribe?"

"Something of the sort." He paused. "Max usually provides a generous pay-off to go with the kiss-off in these situations," he said, looking faintly amused. "It must be a new sensation for him to have to make payment in advance."

Ginny was getting the milk out of the fridge, but his words stopped her in her tracks. She turned to face him.

"You mean—you think Max is trying to *buy* me?" She felt a wave of colour surge into her face. "Oh, no! It just isn't possible. It's too ridiculous."

"Well, perhaps," Toby shrugged, "it's probably not as blatant as that. But he probably senses your hostility and this is in the nature of a sweetener. As I said, they're not usually necessary. It's shaking his ladies off at the end of the affair which Max usually finds most difficult, not the beginning." His smile widened. "And I'd have thought you reminded him too much of Laura for him to want to get involved this time."

"Laura?" She didn't really want to know, but at the same time she couldn't help asking.

"The girl who worked for him in California last year. She was dark and very young as well." Toby paused, then said laconically, "When he told her it was all over, she took an overdose."

"Oh, God!" She was trembling suddenl. "How dreadful. What—what happened?"

"Max found her in time. She was all right after treatment."

"That was lucky."

"Hardly luck. She was in his house, in his bed at the time. He could hardly have missed her."

Ginny made herself reach for the milk and add some to each beaker. She felt stunned and sick, and it was a relief to make her mind, her hands obey her in achieving the mundane and ordinary. The coffee tasted of nothing, and it was scalding hot in her throat, but it dissipated the chill inside her.

Toby was still talking, and she forced herself to concentrate on what he was saying.

"But I'm glad you've developed an immunity to Max. I thought when he told me to stay away that he'd already staked a claim on you."

"No," she managed to say tightly, "no claim at all," and shut out of her mind the memory of that one brutal, troublous kiss. The fact that for a few brief seconds she had been totally aware of her own body, and the demands that physical desire could make on her. She had to resist the impulse to put her hand to her mouth, as if Max's kiss still burned there like a brand for all to see.

"Good." Toby was smiling, drinking his coffee, completely at ease, as if the horrifying little story he had just related was merely commonplace. Which it was perhaps in the kind of world that the Hendrick cousins moved in. Something of what was going on in Ginny's mind must have shown on her face, because he moved suddenly, restively, putting his beaker down.

"Ginny, my sweet, don't look like that. No one's ever overdosed over me, I promise you."

"No, of course not." She tried to smile. "I didn't think for a moment...."

"Good." He smiled at her again. His charm seemed to reach for her, warming her.

She said impulsively, "Oh, Toby, I'm so glad you're here. I'd begun to think you were never going to come down here again."

He said drily, "If Max had had his way, I wouldn't have." He drank the rest of his coffee, then set down the mug. "And now let's go and say hello to your aunt."

As Ginny led the way, it occurred to her that although Toby had accepted her naïve welcome, he had gone no further. Deep inside her she had hoped to hear him say that he'd been unable to stay away a moment longer, that he was as glad to see her as she had confessed she was to see him. She supposed that she had hoped for far too much. Perhaps Toby felt that any such avowals smacked too much of a commitment he was not ready to make. As it was, she seemed to have committed herself, and she wished that she had not been quite so frank about her pleasure in his presence. There were times when she felt painfully gauche, and this was one of them.

Aunt Mary greeted Toby pleasantly, but with a faint reserve which Ginny wished she had copied. Her aunt asked if he had been well, and whether he had been busy since he had last visited his cousin's house. There was a faint stress laid on the last few words, and Toby looked suitably abashed, and hastened to provide her with the explanation he had already given to Ginny. Aunt Mary listened with an impassive face, and when he had finished, murmured a remark which neutrally avoided either sympathy or reproach.

Ginny wondered whether her aunt would offer to allow Toby to stay with them, but she did not, and Ginny did not like to be the first to suggest it.

Besides, she could well imagine Max's reaction when he arrived home to find his cousin installed in their wing, and though she told herself vehemently that his opinions did not weigh with her in the slightest, at the same time she was uneasily aware that that was the merest bravado on her part, and that Max Hendrick had the power to make life very unpleasant for her if she deliberately ignored his wishes.

But not as unpleasant as it had been for that poor girl who had tried to kill herself. Ginny felt a shudder run through her. It would have been so easy, so fatally easy to have been beguiled by Max. She had hardly been prepared to admit even to herself how deeply his kiss had affected her. Oh, it was so easy for him and people like him, she thought bitterly. They could stride through life, using people quite remorselessly, uncaring of the fact that those whom they used might not be strong enough physically or emotionally to withstand the ultimate disillusion.

But she was warned now, and she would never forget that warning, or how near she had been to potential disaster.

Aunt Mary was saying calmly, "Are you on holiday, Toby? We're not used to seeing you in the middle of the week."

He gave a rueful smile. "Hardly a holiday, Miss Clayton. I'm what's known in the theatrical profession as resting. In other words—out of work."

Ginny stared at him, her lips parted in frank astonishment. "You're on the stage?"

"I'm not an actor. I'm a stage designer. Didn't I tell you before?"

"No." She shook her head. "You never said very much at all about your work."

"Perhaps that's because there hasn't been a great deal of it to talk about," he said with wry humour. "At the moment I'm just trying to gain myself a precarious toehold, no more."

Aunt Mary looked a little sceptical. "But surely your cousin as a well-established writer could assist...."

"He could, but he doesn't," Toby said lightly. "And it's my choice. I want to make my own way without Max's patronage. I had enough of that when we were both much younger. I don't even use the Hendrick name for professional purposes. I call myself Toby Christie, which was my mother's name. No one is going to say I made my way up the ladder hanging on to Max's coat tails." He smiled. "It's another thing that hasn't particularly endeared me to him. Max likes to take charge and make everyone dance to his piping, as you may have noticed. It hasn't suited him at all that I want to carve out my own career."

Ginny said in a low voice, "You're very lucky. I—I wish I didn't have to feel obliged to him either."

She felt her aunt's gaze on her in surprise and faint disapproval, but she was unrepentant. She looked at Toby, letting the warmth she saw in his eyes reach out and surround her, feeling the strange little inner ache she had been aware of slowly dissolving away.

She said very clearly and defiantly, "I hate him."

And silently in the loneliness and confusion of her heart, she cried out to Toby, "Love me. Please love me!"

As the days passed, there seemed some sign that her unspoken wish would be granted. Toby seemed in no hurry to return to London and gradually he resumed the happy relationship that he had enjoyed with them all in the early days. This, coupled with Max's continuing absence, would have filled Ginny's cup of joy to the brim if only she had been more certain of what Toby's feelings were towards herself. He still seemed to make very little attempt to try and get her alone.

Perhaps the warmth of her welcome had frightened him off, she thought unhappily, studying herself in the mirror with a critical eye. The trouble was she was so—ordinary, she decided crossly, as her gaze fell on Barbie's photograph. If she tried for a month of Sundays she could never achieve that look of smouldering, tantalising provocation which her sister had managed so effortlessly. Tentatively she experimented, moistening her lips and pouting them slightly, and lowering her eyelids until her thick lashes nearly swept her cheeks, but, she thought sadly, she still didn't look sexy— just bad-tempered.

She giggled and ran a comb through her hair, allowing it to fall round her face in its usual smooth style. She just wasn't the sultry temptress type, and there was no use in pretending anything different. Besides, if Toby was a stage designer, he probably came across hundreds of aspiring actresses cast in that mould. Maybe that was why he liked her, she thought, because she was at least different.

In the meantime, she had his visits to look forward to. She whisked through her daily chores, added Max's mail to the growing pile on his desk, and responded with cheerful insouciance to Mrs. Lanyon's increasingly petulant enquiries about when Max would return.

Ginny was mooching round the kitchen one morning, waiting impatiently for Toby's car to drive in through the gate, when the phone rang.

She felt the oddest sense of dread as she reached out to pick up the receiver. Perhaps it was Toby to say that some work had come up, and he was having to return to London—or even more likely, Max to say that he was on his way back.

"Monk's Dower," she mumbled.

"Is that you, Ginny?" Barbie enquired sharply.

"Yes." Ginny was taken aback. "How are you? Is the play doing well?"

"The play isn't doing at all. It's folded, which is no surprise to anyone," Barbie said crossly. "Don't you ever read the papers?"

"Not the theatrical pages," Ginny admitted. If I had, she thought, I might have heard about Max Hendrick and heard enough to make me run a mile before I agreed to work for him. She forced her mind back to concentrate on what Barbie was saying.

"There's one at eleven-fifteen," her sister's voice came loud and clear. "It should get in around lunchtime, but you can check that from your end. I presume you'll be able to meet me with the car?"

"Meet you where?"

"Oh, for heaven's sake!" Barbie snapped. "Meet me at the station in Market Harford, of course. Haven't you been listening to a word I've been saying? I've just told you I'm coming down for a week or two. The play's folded, and my agent has nothing else in prospect at the moment, and I could do with some relaxation. So can you meet me or can't you?"

Ginny tried to control her whirling thoughts, and to suppress the unworthy feeling of dismay which threatened to overwhelm her. "I—I'll do my best."

"Well, thank you for small mercies, sister dear." Barbie's laugh was mirthless. "I'll see you later, then."

Ginny replaced her own receiver bleakly. This was a development she had not envisaged for a moment. There had not been a word either by letter or telephone from Barbie since the arrival of the photograph, and she had vaguely assumed she was still out on tour somewhere. Now, in a matter of a few hours, she would be here among them, and Ginny didn't really have to ask herself why? Barbie was coming to see if there was a part in the new Max Hendrick play for her.

She sighed. She supposed she really ought to have told her that Max was not here, and wasn't even expected back, but there hadn't been time. No doubt Barbie would be annoyed when she arrived and found her quarry absent.

Aunt Mary was coming downstairs and smiled at her. "Who was that on the telephone, dear?"

"Barbie. She's coming down for a few days."

"Well, it will be very pleasant to see her again and hear all her news," Aunt Mary said robustly, after a brief pause.

Ginny managed a smile. "I'm afraid the news isn't awfully good. The play she was in has come off, and she's out of work."

"But not for long, I'm sure. Such a pretty girl," said Aunt Mary with scrupulous fairness. "There'll be plenty of other plays."

"Oh, yes." Ginny bit her lip. "Including the one I'm working on. I'm sure that's the main reason she's coming—to meet Max Hendrick. That's probably why she sent that awful picture too—to prepare the ground. Well, thank heavens he isn't here—although what she'll say when I break that little bit of bad news...."

"Oh, but he is here, dear," said Aunt Mary. "I was just coming to tell you. I felt sure you hadn't heard the car arrive."

Ginny groaned, "Oh lord, that's all I need!"

All the same she felt quite pleased with herself as she presented herself at the study a minute or two later. If he'd arrived unexpectedly in order to catch her out again, then he had failed. The house was clean, and his work was done. So she was totally unprepared for the grim look which greeted her as she entered.

"Good morning," she said pointedly. "Did you have a successful trip?"

"Reasonably." There was no mistaking the anger, icily controlled in his voice. "And have you managed to keep yourself occupied in my absence?"

Her heart sank. So he knew about Toby, and wasn't pleased.

Her own temper rising, she said sharply, "As long as I do my work to your satisfaction, Mr. Hendrick, I'd say my free time was my own affair, wouldn't you?"

"It isn't your free time that concerns me." His tone was biting. He pointed to the desk. "This is the mail, is it? Collected presumably by you—but not opened."

"You didn't tell me to open it," she protested uneasily. There was something very wrong here, but she was at a loss to know what it was.

"Not even when it's addressed to yourself—and marked 'Urgent?'" He picked up two large packets from the desk and weighed them speculatively in his hands.

"Addressed to me?" she repeated. She looked at the packets he was holding, and saw her own name printed boldly on their labels. "But what are they?"

"Work, oddly enough." He threw them down on the desk with a thud. "The revisions which have arisen as a result of the conference, and a complete re-working of Act Two. Both items which I expected to be completed and waiting for me today. I only came to fetch them and some other papers. I intended to return to London tonight. Now it looks as if I'm in for a long wait."

Ginny longed for the floor to open and engulf her, but it didn't. It remained as hard and unyielding as Max's face.

He said impatiently, "I pay you to use your initiative, Ginevra. Didn't you even read the addresses on the letters before you brought them in here? What in hell's the matter with you? Are you in love or something?''

His eyes narrowed as he watched the hot colour flood into her pale cheeks. He said softly, ''So that's it! Toby's back in town. I might have known. All I can say is that for both your sakes, he'd better not be staying here.''

''No, he isn't.'' She lifted her chin defiantly. ''You made your views on that perfectly clear. He's staying at a hotel in Market Harford.''

''Is he now?'' His voice was grim. ''We'll see about that!''

She said on a high breathless note, ''But I want him to stay. It—it's me that he's come to see. It's none of your business. As long as he doesn't get in your way, what difference does it make to you?''

''It's already made quite a difference to me.'' Max gestured at the desk. ''He seems to have had a disastrous effect on your wits as well as your heart.''

Her flush deepened. ''Again, that's none of your business. I—I'm sorry I didn't realise you'd be sending me work. I suppose you'll want to engage some extra help to get all the typing done in time.'' She thrust a shaking hand into the pocket of her skirt and drew out the crumpled envelope which Toby had given her when he first arrived. She had carried it round with her always, quite deliberately. ''You'd better have this back to pay for it.''

She flung it at his feet. Max looked down at it for a long moment, his dark face unreadable, then he gave her a long measuring look.

''Where did you get this?''

''Toby brought it for me.'' She gave him a look of dislike. ''You may not want him to come down here, but it doesn't stop you using him as a messenger. Perhaps you thought your money would be more acceptable to me if it came from him. Well, it isn't.''

''Apparently not.'' He still made no attempt to retrieve the envelope. ''Are you trying to tell me that all the work you've done for me so far has been—I hesitate to say—for love?''

"No, I don't," she said hotly. "But I'm not a charity case, and I refuse to be treated as if I was. We agreed what my salary was to be, and this is way above our agreement. I only want what I'm entitled to."

"At the moment," he said slowly, "I'm thinking in terms of a damned good hiding."

Ginny took an apprehensive step backwards. "Don't you dare lay a finger on me!"

"I've no intention of touching you," he said with a kind of weary contempt. "But I do want to know why you're behaving as if your salary had turned into some kind of— immoral earnings. I told you I intended to pay you extra for helping with that dinner party. You agreed. Why change your mind now?"

"It's too much," she muttered defensively.

"I don't agree, but far be it for me to argue with a lady," he said derisively. He bent and picked up the envelope between his fingers as if it was something distasteful, then he tore it into small pieces which he fed into the waste basket beside the desk. "Satisfied?" he enquired, too pleasantly. "Meanwhile...." He reached into an inside pocket and produced a wallet. As Ginny watched he peeled off a number of notes which he laid down on the desk in front of her. He said unemotionally, "I think that meets the letter of our agreement exactly. And an extra fiver for the dinner, if your churlish little mind won't accept any more." His lip curled for a moment as he tossed another five-pound note on top of the pile. He said smoothly, "And that's for the kiss, darling."

He shrugged off his coat and dropped it on to the chair.

"As I've decided to stay, some coffee might be in order. You might see to it while I make some phone calls."

Ginny turned and went towards the door like an automaton.

He said, "Take your money with you, Ginevra."

He was sitting on the edge of the desk as she turned unwillingly, and already reaching for the extension. He looked relaxed and very much in control of the situation, and although she longed to refuse, she did not dare. What was worse, she had to lean across him to pick up the money. All in all, it was one of the most shaming things which had ever happened to her, she thought, her face burning as she got outside.

She was waiting for the kettle to boil when she heard someone call her name from the kitchen door, and turning, she saw Toby smiling at her.

She returned the smile, but with constraint.

"What's the matter, love?" He advanced into the kitchen. "Afraid the ogre will catch us together?"

"Don't be silly." But she kept her voice low. "But he isn't very pleased with me. He—he sent me some work to do which I overlooked—somehow...."

Toby said, "Perhaps you had other things on your mind." His eyes were quizzical suddenly, and Ginny turned away concentrating rather fiercely on her coffee-making, afraid that he might read her feelings too easily.

"You look pale," he said after a moment. "Has Max started slave-driving you already?"

"I'm not a slave," she said. "I do get paid. By the way—" there had been something nagging at her, a niggling inconsistency "—why did Max give you my salary to bring down? After all, you told me he didn't want you to come here, and it was clear he hadn't expected you—so...?"

"Ah," Toby's face was mischievous. "He didn't precisely give it to me. I think that was the last thing he had in mind, but he'd written your name on the envelope and was obviously intending to post it, so I thought I'd save him the trouble. See?"

"Not really." She felt weary suddenly and oddly dispirited. "I don't really understand why you have come down—or was it just to annoy Max?"

"Hardly. I came to see you, little Ginny." There was a caress in his voice, and her heart was thumping painfully as she heard it. "As it is—"his tone was rueful"—I've been called back to London. I'm in line for some work, and it's too good a chance to miss. But I'll be back in a fortnight, and I'll see you then. Max can't keep you working all the time, so one evening I'll have you all to myself. We'll have dinner—go dancing perhaps. Is it a date?"

Her eyes shone. "It's a date. Oh, Toby, it'll be wonderful!"

"Not exactly wonderful, sweetie. I doubt whether the local night spots have much to recommend them, but we can live in hope. Besides, I owe you for all the hospitality I've enjoyed here."

Ginny wished he hadn't said that. Somehow it took some of the glitter from this wonderful, shining invitation. She didn't want him to take her out because he was grateful or because she'd been hospitable. She wanted him to take her out because that was what he wanted too. She wanted more than gratitude or a sense of obligation, much more.

He reached out a hand and stroked her cheek gently, and she stood motionless, coffee jar in hand, feeling thrilled and foolish at the same time.

"Think of me sometimes," he urged gently, and she stared down at the worktop, knowing she would be unable to think of anyone or anything else and frightened that he would see it in her eyes.

When he had gone, she put the mugs of coffee on a tray and carried them back to the study. Max was still on the telephone and she guessed from the warm, intimate note in his voice that he was talking to a woman, and wondered if it was Vivien Lanyon and he was giving her all the reassurances that she craved.

She set the coffee down, and picked up the two packets which had been addressed to her, avoiding Max's rather mocking look as she did so. She carried them over to her table, and slit them open, unable to avoid a slight whistle of dismay as she saw how much there was for her to do. She glanced at her watch. She would have to make the typewriter burst into flames if she was to complete a respectable amount before begging some time off to go and meet Barbie at the station.

She heard the tinkle as Max's receiver was replaced, then

he said softly, "What's the matter, Ginevra? Parting for lovers is supposed to be such sweet sorrow, or hadn't you heard?"

He was laughing at her, although his face was impassive, and she guessed that he must have seen Toby's car from his window.

She said, and her voice quivered, "I hate you, Max Hendrick!"

He lifted one shoulder in a shrug. "That's your privilege, sweetheart. Your job is to do my typing, and that's all I require of you, so let's keep emotions out of it, shall we?"

She stood stiff and still, looking across the room at him, then she said quietly, "Perhaps before I start, I could make a phone call. I have to arrange for a taxi to meet my sister from the train. I'd intended to go myself, but...."

"But my inconvenient return put paid to all your plans for the day," he completed the sentence for her smoothly. "There's no need to get a taxi. I'll collect her for you, if you feel it's a problem."

She was about to say, "But you don't know her," but bit it back in time, because she wasn't at all sure of her ground.

She said unwillingly, "Thank you. Are you sure it won't be too much trouble?"

He slanted a look at her. "If it's the lady of the photograph, no trouble at all," he drawled.

She said hurriedly, "If you pick her up at the station, then I can use my lunch break to get her room ready—our room that is. She'll be sharing with me," she added wildly, apropos nothing at all, and flushed at Max's sardonic look.

"How very sisterly, Ginevra. And precisely who is supposed to be chaperoning whom?"

"I don't think chaperons are necessary nowadays." She picked up paper and carbons and fed them into her machine with hands which shook a little. She was annoyed that she had been lured into this kind of personal conversation again, although she supposed that there was little more personal than telling someone that you hated them, which she'd done only a few minutes since.

She said sharply and without thinking, "Barbie is her own mistress," and could have bitten her tongue out, because that was the last remark she should have made if her suspicions had any foundation whatsoever.

Max said drily, "You mean she does as she likes? That's not quite the same thing, Ginevra."

"You know what I mean," she muttered, staring at the typewriter keys.

"Yes." He got up restlessly. "So that's settled, then. You prepare the sisterly bower and make sure the welcome mat is at the door, and I'll meet the train."

She nodded without speaking, and began to type as if her life depended on it. Much later she stole a glance at him. He was sitting, staring at a letter he had just opened, but she knew instinctively that his mind was not on it. What was he thinking about? she wondered, as she began to type. His face had looked sardonic and slightly bitter. Perhaps he was regretting his offer to meet Barbie at the station. Or perhaps he was cynically congratulating himself on having arranged a private reunion with an old flame under the guise of an act of kindness.

Kindness. She stabbed viciously at a wrong key and had to stop to make a fiddling alteration. There was no kindness in him, only self-interest, and she must never let herself forget it.

"I hate him. I hate him," she told herself under her breath, her vehemence warring with an odd feeling of desolation which could only be for Toby.

CHAPTER SIX

Two weeks had never dragged past so slowly, Ginny thought miserably as the second of them drew to its close. Her working relationship with Max had deteriorated to an extent where it could only be described as a state of armed neutrality. He seemed now to speak to her only when necessary, and Toby's name was never mentioned by either of them in any connection.

Not that there had been much time for personal conversation. Ginny had worked herself almost to a blur in an effort to reduce the backlog of work. Then there had been the new pages of dialogue which Max dictated to her to transcribe. It was almost the sole communication between them—his voice putting words into other people's mouths.

There were visitors too. The interrupted series of meetings in London were continued at Monk's Dower, and Ginny was able to take her typewriter into the dining room and work there in peace for a few days. There were contracts to sign, and sums of money were mentioned which made her blink. After the visitors in their dark City suits had departed, she had asked diffidently if she could continue to work in the dining room on her own, but had received so definite a negative that she had not dared make an issue of it.

Besides, she did not want to arouse his anger. He was totally and utterly committed to the last act that he was writing, even to the extent of taking the phone off the hook so that he should not be disturbed by daytime calls. Often in the evenings, she saw the study light burning until late, and knew that the following day there would be pages of rewriting for her to type. But she didn't mind. She had never minded the work. And as long as Max regarded her simply as a pair of efficient hands operating a typewriter, she could cope with him too.

She was not simply working hard for Max, however. When she returned to her own part of the house in the evening, there was cooking and housework awaiting her, and often she was bone-weary when she finally fell into bed in the room which she now shared with Barbie.

"Shared" was not perhaps the right word, she thought wryly, as she contemplated the complete take-over of the limited wardrobe space, the ousting of her things from the dressing table drawers, and the overspill of Barbie's possessions on to every available surface. Her sister seemed to have brought far more clothes with her than were necessary for a couple of weeks' break, and although nothing had been said, Ginny had begun to suspect that Barbie might be planning a much longer stay.

And if the purpose of her visit had been the captivation of Max Hendrick, then she would have to stay longer, because on the past two weeks' showing, she had enjoyed little success.

Barbie had glittered with complacency on her arrival. "Clever of you, darling," she had laughed, bestowing a careless kiss somewhere in the region of Ginny's left cheek. "How did you know that was exactly what I wanted?"

"It wasn't altogether my idea," Ginny returned drily, and Barbie laughed, pushing back her mane of red-gold hair.

"Better and better! I knew it was a good idea to send that picture. He did see it, of course."

"Of course." Ginny gave her a quick look. "But hadn't you met before?"

"No." Barbie's surprised glance seemed genuine enough. "I don't, unfortunately, move in those kinds of exalted circles. Besides, I've far more chance of making an impression here in this backwater where there's no competition." She let the tip of her tongue appear between her teeth. "Max Hendrick is exactly my kind of man."

"You're not the only one with that opinion—even in this backwater." Ginny tried to speak lightly. "Mrs. Lanyon who happens to be my employer shares your view, and she has the prior claim."

"Had, darling." Barbie gave a dazzling smile. "Let's use the past tense for the married lady, shall we?"

"She's a widow."

"Then she'll just have to find someone else to be merry with." There was a distinct edge to Barbie's voice. "The dishy Mr. Hendrick is about to transfer his attentions, and I expect his affections to follow—right?"

But Barbie's expectations had so far remained unfulfilled. She had not, Ginny supposed, bargained for Max's total absorption in his work, or realised how little their paths might cross, even if they were living in the same house. And she was frankly displeased when Ginny refused point-blank to invite her quarry to dinner or to lunch on Sunday.

On the few occasions that she had encountered him, she had employed all the considerable weapons at her command and flirted outrageously with him, much to Aunt Mary's unspoken disapproval. But that was as far as it went. Max made no secret of the fact that he admired her, and he was quite prepared to take part in the kind of sophisticated badinage that Barbie enjoyed, but the invitation she had confidently counted on was not forthcoming, and her temper had become correspondingly shorter as the days passed. By the end of the first week she had reduced Tim to mutinous silence and Aunt Mary to avidly offended monosyllables. Ginny, tired herself and irritated by Barbie's self-centred grumbling, found herself all too often in the role of peacemaker.

Sometimes, she thought half-humorously, half in despair, she wished she had been on really good terms with Max so that she could have said to him, laughing, "When are you going to put my sister out of her misery and take her out to dinner, so that we can all have some peace?"

But that was impossible, and she felt instinctively anyway that where Barbie was concerned, Max knew exactly what he was doing, and that the mocking deference he showed her was all perfectly calculated.

"But, how I wish they'd go and play their games elsewhere," Ginny muttered crossly.

Barbie was not the only one who did not know where she stood with a man, she was being forced to realise. Toby had not written or telephoned since his return to London, and she was beginning to wonder, rather forlornly, whether the promised dinner date had been totally dismissed from his mind. Perhaps keeping the women in their lives dangling on a string was a Hendrick family trait, she thought with a sigh.

She tried to console herself with the rather bleak reflection that her wardrobe did not really contain anything suitable for the kind of evening Toby had suggested anyway. A long cotton skirt, and a V-necked black sweater, neither of them new, were about as much as she ran to, and she had already considered and discounted the idea of buying a new dress. Tim was shooting up in height all the time, and would need new school trousers and shirts very soon, not to mention pocket money for the French trip which was looming nearer all the time.

The financial position wasn't helped by the presence of another mouth to feed. Barbie had announced soon after her arrival that because she was out of work she wouldn't be able to contribute to the family budget, but this hadn't affected her extravagant consumption of hot water or the fact that she was constantly on the telephone either to her agent or friends in London. When a mild remonstrance from Ginny had led to an accusation that she was turning into a miser, she had said no more.

Besides, there were other accusations when Barbie was in a bad mood that were even harder to bear. Claims that she did not have her sister's best interests at heart, or that she had deliberately put a spoke in her wheel for fear of offending Vivien Lanyon or because she wanted Max herself.

"That's ridiculous, and you know it," Ginny said wearily one night as they were getting ready for bed.

"Is it?" Barbie's eyes glittered as she surveyed her sister.

"All I know is that he was interested, definitely interested, and now—nothing."

"He's very busy," Ginny offered as a palliative. "He isn't seeing Mrs. Lanyon either, as far as I know."

"But he does see you—every day," Barbie said silkily. "Perhaps there's a dark horse in this race after all."

"I'm his typist, no more, no less," Ginny protested. "And that's the way we both want it. Besides...." She paused abruptly, aware that she had been about to give herself away. She hadn't mentioned Toby's existence to her sister, although there had been plenty of opportunities to do so, but she was conscious of an odd inexplicable reluctance, and the longer she kept silent, the more impossible the subject became to mention casually.

"Besides what?" Barbie's eyes were sharp with interest now. "Besides, there's someone else? Don't tell me some rustic swain has actually taken your fancy? Amazing! I'd always written you down as one of the worst cases of arrested virginity I'd ever seen."

Ginny swallowed. She supposed she could laugh and say, "Well, actually it's Max's cousin..." as if the relationship was a settled thing. But she wasn't sure she could cope with that kind of pretense. Her feelings for Toby were too new, and too uncertain and fragile, to be exposed to the real possibility of Barbie's mockery.

"He's neither rustic, nor my swain." She tried for a light tone.

"So there is someone," Barbie remarked amusedly. "And you're being secretive about it, so it's serious."

"No, it isn't." The betraying blush which rose in her cheeks made a nonsense of Ginny's denial. "We—we just see each other when he comes down here, that's all. But we've never been out together," she added.

"I'm not altogether surprised. You've never been a raving beauty, darling, but you don't even make the best of yourself. Look at yourself now! I know for a fact that you had that denim skirt while you were still at school, and that shirt has seen better days too."

"It will have to see worse ones before I've finished with it." Ginny tried to speak cheerfully. "I haven't the time or the money to spend on my appearance that you have, Barbie—nor the raw material to work on," she added fairly.

Barbie accepted the compliment with a lift of her shoulder. "But that still is no excuse for going around as if you were dressed by Oxfam," she complained. "Surely there must be times when this guy's around when you want to look decent."

"Yes, there are," said Ginny, unable to repress a little sigh. "But there's nothing I can do about it, so what can't be cured must be endured, as Aunt Mary says."

Barbie shuddered artistically. "For God's sake don't start quoting the old witch! It's bad enough having to sit and listen to her rambling on about the good old days every evening."

"She's getting old," Ginny said gently. "And old people like to look back on the past."

"And if you're not careful, that's exactly where you'll be. In the past with her." Barbie sat up energetically. "Does this man of yours give advance warning of his arrival? It might be fun to work on you a bit and surprise him. There must be something among the gear I've brought which would fit you. We're almost the same size, even if we're not the same shape."

"Oh, Barbie, would you?" Ginny bit her lip. "He did say he was going to take me out to dinner quite soon, but I've heard nothing since and . . . ."

"Probably terrified you'd turn up in that skirt," Barbie remarked unkindly. "And what's the name of this reluctant Casanova?"

"Well, you might have heard of him, actually." Ginny began to brush her hair. "He's in stage design, although he's not working at the moment, and his name's Toby— Toby Christie. But that's not his real name, because really he's Max's cousin." She waited for some comment from Barbie, but there was silence. She swung around on the dressing stool and looked at her sister who had been manicuring her nails, but who was now leaning back against her pillow staring at her hands as if she had never seen them before. "Have you heard of him, Barbie? Is something the matter?"

"No, nothing at all. I thought I'd broken a nail, but all's well. And I may have heard of your friend, but frankly—" Barbie gave a little shrug"—one meets so many people."

"Yes," Ginny agreed, sobered for a moment by an inevitable comparison between Barbie's world and her own limited prospects, "I suppose you do."

Ginny did not sleep well that night. Tired though she was, her mind was a prey to conflicting thoughts and emotions, but none of them seemed to make any coherent pattern in her weary brain. Barbie seemed restless too, and Ginny, doing her best to lie still and not disturb her sister further, wondered if insomnia was catching. When at last she did fall asleep shortly before dawn, her rest was invaded by dreams, not memorable in themselves but leaving vague recollections of uneasiness as she dragged herself unwillingly out of bed the next day.

Max was already at work when she presented herself in the study. He looked up as she came in with a muttered apology for being slightly late. His glance sharpened slightly as he observed her wan appearance and shadowed eyes, but he made no comment.

It was only when she screwed up the third ruined sheet and hurled it into the waste basket beside her that he said abruptly, "Are you finding all this too much for you, Ginevra?"

"What do you mean?"

She turned to stare at him in immediate apprehension and saw his firm lips tighten.

"All this work I expect you to do." His voice was impatient. "The house is immaculate, apart from all the typing and retyping I pile on to you all the time. Do you want me to make some alternative arrangements?"

"Has Mrs. Lanyon been talking to you?" An indignant flush rose in her cheeks.

"No," he said drily. "What gives you that idea?"

Ginny shrugged. "I—formed the impression she didn't think much of my services."

"I don't think she takes quite the consuming interest in my domestic arrangements that you seem to think. And I suspect that there are undercurrents here I'd prefer not to become entangled in just now." There was open amusement in his voice now, and her flush deepened defensively. "But she's heard no complaints from me, I promise you."

Ginny was about to say hotly, "No, and that's probably the whole point. She'd prefer it if you found fault with me." But the unwisdom of any such remark presented itself so forcefully that she remained silent.

She began to assemble a new batch of paper and carbons. "Well, I have no complaints either," she said at last as she began to type.

"I'm delighted to hear it," he said ironically. "Also a little surprised." He was silent for a moment, and the tension hung between them, almost tangible in the stillness. Ginny heard herself swallow.

Max said almost gently, "But to get back to the point under discussion, Ginny, are you finding the combination of jobs too much for you? You've been looking tired, lately—strained."

But how do you know, she thought, when you hardly ever look at me, and when you do, you don't really seem to see me? Something of what she was thinking must have shown on her face, because he said swiftly, "I'm not blind, you know, Ginevra." And there was a note in his voice which she did not wholly understand, and her eyes met his, startled and disturbed, and their gazes met and locked for a moment longer than time....

Then his brows rose and the mocking smile she so much detested played around the corners of his mouth, and he said softly and jibingly, "So what's the problem, Ginevra? Unrequited love for Toby?"

"That's none of your business," she flashed stormily. "Oh, why can't you leave me alone?"

"I thought that's what I had been doing."

"Well, I don't want to talk about Toby."

"It's not a subject we'd be likely to agree on, I admit. But you keep straying from the point, my child."

She said in a stifled voice, "I can manage the work perfectly well, thank you. Does that satisfy you?"

"No," he said coldly. "But I can see it's all the answer I'm going to get. You really don't trust me, do you, Ginevra?"

She bent her head. "Have I any reason to?"

Max's mouth twisted slightly. "Again, we probably wouldn't agree."

It was almost a relief when the study door opened, although Barbie was the last person in the world she had expected to see smiling in the doorway.

Her sister said coolly, "I hope I'm not interrupting anything vital, but Ginny's wanted on the telephone."

"You're not interrupting a thing." Max got courteously to his feet. "Ginny and I were pursuing a singularly profitless debate. You'd better run along and take your call, if it's so important," he added to her, and she nodded and rose to her feet.

As she closed the study door and turned away, she heard Barbie laugh, and she wondered what Max had said, and if the joke had been about her.

The curious feeling of confusion and hurt which her conversation with Max and its aftermath had engendered lent an edge to her tone as she picked up the receiver and gave her name.

"Ginny, my sweet, did you think I'd forgotten all about you?"

"Oh, Toby!" Her voice lifted in delight. "I—I didn't know what to think." All thoughts of dissimulation far from her mind, she cradled the receiver happily in hands which shook a little.

"I had the chance of some work," he said casually, "so I had to chase around a bit—produce some drawings—you know the sort of thing."

She didn't but she agreed anyway.

"Anyway, I'm free now, and I'll be down in Market Harford later on today. You haven't made any plans for this evening?"

"Well—no," she stammered, her pleasure at the thought of seeing him warring with a feminine desire not to be too readily available.

"Wonderful!" There was an undercurrent of laughter in his voice as if he could sense her confusion. "I've already booked a table for us at Les Deux Etrangers at Wishlade, so you can see I was counting on you, Ginny mine. I'll pick you up around half seven. Right?"

"I'll look forward to it," she said primly, aware of how much she'd let slip already, remembering the last time she had seen him.

"Sweetheart, you're priceless! Tonight, then."

She replaced the phone slowly. He'd called her "Ginny mine" and "sweetheart." Were these just casual endearments, such as Barbie sprinkled indiscriminately into the conversation or were they really signs of the deeper commitment she was hoping for?

Aunt Mary was coming down the stairs as she turned away. "Who was that on the telephone, my dear? More of Barbara's theatrical friends?"

"Not this time." Ginny's smile shone. "It was Toby. He's taking me out to dinner tonight."

"I see. Well, that all sounds very pleasant." Aunt Mary's tone was surprisingly non-committal. "And I shall enjoy meeting Toby once again."

Ginny went reluctantly back to the study. Barbie, she knew, would regard her return as an intrusion. She had no doubt that if Toby's phone call had not occurred so fortuitously, her sister would have found some other excuse to seek her out during working hours and thrust herself upon Max's notice once again.

But as she stepped through the dividing door, it was to see Barbie coming towards her, and clearly in a good temper. She was humming a little tune and the smile on her lips suggested a cat that had not only licked the cream but made inroads into the milk as well.

"There's an obedient little secretary," she remarked as she saw Ginny. "I've been keeping him sweet for you, darling. He's actually quite easy to manage, if you know the right way to go about it."

Ginny tried to return the smile. "And you think you do?"

"Sure of it, sweetie." Barbie gave a little laugh. "I—really—do you think I could be on my way. Think of it, Mouse! A solid London run, and then possibly Broadway, courtesy of Max Hendrick Sure-Fire-Hits Limited. All I have to do is play my cards right." She gave Ginny a swift glance. "Well, you could at least look pleased for me."

"Barbie, nothing's happened yet."

"Haven't I just told you, it's just beginning, starting off with drinks tonight. I won't waste my chances." Her eyes sharpened a little, "And what about your little romance?"

"I'm being taken out to dinner this evening." Ginny paused. "Did you mean what you said, Barbie—about lending me a dress and things?"

"Of course, I'll go and look through a few possibilities now." Barbie patted her cheek carelessly in passing with one well-manicured hand. There was an almost feverish glitter about her which worried Ginny a little as she walked down the passage. She could allow Barbie a measure of triumph for the success of her strategy. After all, she'd achieved the invitation from Max which she'd wanted, but there was an intensity about her that Ginny could not understand.

She avoided Max's sardonic stare as she went across to her desk and sat down.

"You still look miserable," he remarked after a moment or two. "What's the matter, Ginevra? Isn't the achievement of your heart's desire all that it's cracked up to be? I presume the urgent phone call was from Toby?"

"Yes, it was," she said baldly. "He's taking me out this evening. We're going to a restuarant called Les Deux Etrangers. I expect you know it well."

"I've been there."

"Naturally. Well, tonight I'm going there. Unless you object, of course," she added with heavy irony.

"Not in the slightest," he said. "The food is excellent. You should enjoy it."

There was open amusement in his voice, and she sat rigidly, glaring at the typewriter, despising herself for having tried to force a confrontation between them, and hating him for thwarting her.

Her heart's desire, she thought. That was exactly what she was achieving. It was going to be the most wonderful evening of her life, and nothing Max could say or do was going to spoil it or make the slightest difference.

SOME hours later Ginny stood staring at her mirrored reflection with a feeling of utter disbelief. A stranger looked back at her, a stranger whose mysteriously shadowed eyes were deepened from hazel to green by the drift of jade chiffon she wore, whose mouth glowed, and whose eyelids were frosted with silver. Her hands stole up to touch her bare throat. Her shoulders were bare too except for the narrow shoestring straps of the dress, tied in soft bows. Her skin looked pearl-white, except for the faint flush along the cheekbones where Barbie's expert fingers had applied blusher, and the delicacy of her bone structure was enhanced by the styling of her hair which had been piled up on top of her head in a soft swirl, with only a few loose tendrils allowed to curl round her ears and the nape of her neck.

She swallowed, pulling at the filmy material of her dress with nervous fingers.

"Barbie, I can't wear this! It's far too expensive. Suppose I tore it—spilled something...."

"Then you'll have to have it mended or cleaned." Her sister did not even look up, apparently completely absorbed in varnishing the perfect ovals of her nails. "Anyway, I don't like the dress. Buying it was a mistake. It's far too young and ingenuous for me."

Ginny stared at her, puzzled by the odd bitterness in her

voice, then turned back to the mirror for another look at herself.

"I hardly recognise myself," she confessed.

"Wasn't that the whole purpose of the exercise?" Barbie enquired curtly.

Ginny bit her lip. Barbie had been in an odd mood that evening, or rather in an odd fluctuation of moods. At times she had seemed quite animated and enthusiastic, choosing dresses at random from the wardrobe, then throwing the rejects across the bed. She had worked on Ginny's make-up and hair like an artist putting the finishing touches to a portrait, in spite of Ginny's laughing protests. Then next moment her behaviour seemed to suggest that she was regretting her generous impulses, and resenting the time and trouble she was taking. But why? Ginny wondered, with a little suppressed sigh. Perhaps her lack of sophistication was irritating to her sister, or maybe she had decided that dressing her up for the evening was just a game which she had tired of, just as she had tired of the games they had played together as children.

"I can't thank you enough," she tried again.

"Oh, don't fuss so much! It's been quite amusing to see if I could make you look decent for once. You could be quite attractive if you took the trouble."

Ginny picked up the crocheted white shawl which had been Aunt Mary's last birthday present to her, and slipped it round her shoulders. It felt warm and comforting, which was more than could be said for Barbie's last remark, she thought, wincing inwardly, especially when she had managed to convince herself that the stranger in the mirror was more than just "quite attractive."

"I think I heard someone at the door." She picked up the small green kid bag which exactly matched the wispy sandals Barbie had loaned her.

"Well, don't be in too much of a hurry to rush downstairs," Barbie advised. "Absence makes the heart grow fonder, you know." She stood up and stretched slightly, then wandered forward to take Ginny's place in front of

the mirror. There was a voluptuousness about her which
the wispy half-cup bra and lace-trimmed waist slip she was
wearing only accentuated, and as Ginny watched her
uncertainly, she ran her hands over her waist and hips,
half caressingly, half in amusement, then smiled compla-
cently. The smile widened, as her eyes met Ginny's in the
mirror.

"Just checking on my stock in trade, darling," she said
lightly. "I wouldn't want the lively Max to be disappointed
in any way. And for heaven's sake stop looking so prim
and disapproving—as if you were about to start reading me
some Victorian tract on morality! I don't need it, I assure
you. I know what I'm doing, and where I'm going."

"Perhaps," Ginny said soberly. "But you don't really
know Max Hendrick."

Barbie's eyes flashed. "And you do, I suppose? Honestly, Ginny, who are you trying to kid? Well, thanks for
the pious little warning, darling, but I promise you I don't
need it."

Ginny sighed inaudibly. For a moment she had been
tempted to tell Barbie about the girl Laura in California.
Perhaps she too had known where she was going and what
she was doing, until the day when heartbreak and despair
caught up with her at Max's hands. But what use would it
have been? Ginny had a shrewd idea her sister would only
have shrugged the sordid little story away as no concern of
hers.

"But it's a concern of mine," Ginny thought hotly as she
went down the stairs. "And that's why I can't let myself
like him or trust him."

The hall below was in darkness, but light shone out of the
sitting room where she could hear Aunt Mary enquiring
courteously, "Would you care for a sherry? I'm sure my
niece will be down in a moment."

She called out, "I'm here," and waited on the staircase
smiling, wanting Toby to walk out into the hall and see her
there, groomed and beautiful for him.

The sitting room door swung open and the hall was

flooded with light dazzling her for a moment, so that she closed her eyes involuntarily.

She said, "Honestly!" and opened her eyes, the laughing protest dying on her lips as she saw Max standing at the foot of the stairs looking up at her, his face inscrutable as if she were indeed the stranger she had fancied herself to be.

For a moment she could have cried out with rejection and disappointment. It was all too painfully reminiscent of that other moment weeks ago when she had walked into the kitchen at Monk's Dower and seen him standing there, dark and dangerous and alien.

She said huskily, "I thought— that is, I was expecting it to be Toby."

"I'm aware of that," he said coolly. "And I was expecting it to be your sister."

She came down the stairs slowly, because the heels of the pretty sandals were slightly higher than she was used to, very conscious of him there, leaning against the wall by the sitting room door, watching her with that unreadable expression in his eyes.

"Barbie's not quite ready." She wanted to break the awkward silence which was developing. "She—she's been helping me."

"So I can see." He stood back to allow her to precede him into the sitting room where Aunt Mary was pouring sherry, and Tim looked up from the television long enough to whistle briefly before becoming absorbed in his programme again.

"That's a charming colour, my dear." Aunt Mary gave a brisk nod as she surveyed Ginny. "Don't you think so, Max?"

"Charming." His voice was dry. "But it isn't my opinion which matters to Ginevra, Miss Clayton."

"Nonsense." Aunt Mary's glance as she handed him his sherry was slightly repressive. "All young girls enjoy receiving compliments. Isn't that so, Ginny?"

Ginny murmured something, feeling her face flame with embarrassment. Oh, where was Toby? Why didn't he come? She sipped hastily at the sherry her great-aunt had given her and almost choked. She was uneasily aware that Max was still watching her, probably amused at her ineptitude, and she wished fervently she had remained upstairs safe from his mocking scrutiny.

She had to endure fifteen minutes of it before Toby eventually arrived with profuse apologies for his lateness. He was clearly taken aback to find Max in the sitting room ahead of him, and the two men exchanged cool greetings.

Ginny could have stamped her foot. This wasn't at all how she had visualised the start of her evening. Toby had barely glanced at her when he had come in; his attention had been riveted by his cousin's presence. And now he was clearly impatient to be gone. No more impatient than she was, she thought, draining her sherry and setting down the glass. Once they were alone together, everything would be all right.

They moved out into the hall. Aunt Mary followed, chatting amiably about the weather and the likelihood of a slight frost that night, with Max close behind her.

Barbie was just coming down the stairs. She was wearing a violet dress, its wrap-around style moulding itself to every inch of her shapely figure, and her hair stood out like a gleaming aureole about her head. Her lips and nails were as crimson as a banner, and she was smiling. It was the perfect entrance, and she was playing it for all she was worth. Even Ginny could recognise that.

She said lightly, "Just off, darling? Have a wonderful time." She smiled across Ginny's head at Toby. "Take care of my little sister."

He said, "I'll do that. How are you, Barbie? It's good to see you again."

"Life couldn't be better, darling." Barbie descended the last few stairs and went towards Max with her hands outstretched, her eyes meeting and holding his with practised assurance.

"Have I kept you waiting?" Her voice took on a lower pitch. It was warm and intimate suddenly.

"It was all worth waiting for." He lifted one of the hands she gave him to his lips.

Ginny felt her own arm suddenly gripped by Toby. "Come on, love," he said tersely. "We'd better get going, or we shall be late."

He didn't speak much on the journey, but Ginny attributed this to the fact that Wishlade wasn't the easiest place in the world to find. The lanes which led to it were rambling and none too wide, and she was thankful that he was concentrating on his driving.

The restaurant, when they arrived, turned out to be two converted cottages, low-roofed and heavily timbered. After Toby had parked the car they went into the bar, a long, low-ceilinged room, furnished in a traditional style, with a log fire blazing at one end of it. There were a number of other would-be diners already ensconced, with aperitifs, studying menus, and the room was filled with talk and laughter.

Toby fetched Ginny another sherry and ordered a vodka and tonic for himself. As he joined her at the table, he smiled at her.

"Have I told you how lovely you look?"

She felt herself thrill with pleasure at the warmth in his voice and smile.

"It's none of my doing really," she confessed. "Even the dress belongs to my sister." She paused. "I suppose I shouldn't have told you that. I should have shrugged, and said, 'What, in this old thing?'"

He was laughing. "I prefer your own answer. And the dress is far more your style than your sister's."

She said doubtfully, "Yes, I suppose you know about these things through your work."

"Partly." He lifted his glass and drank. "But I've got eyes like any other man."

Ginny stared down at her sherry. "I—I didn't realise you knew Barbie. She didn't seem to recognise your name when I mentioned it to her."

He shrugged. "In the theatre, you meet so many people.

Besides, your sister is rather memorable, unlike myself.''

She said shyly, "I think you're memorable, Toby."

"And I think you're delightful." He handed her a menu. "Shall we sort out what we're going to have to eat?"

It was an extensive list and most of it was in French, but many of the dishes were accompanied by a brief description in English which helped. Everything sounded mouthwatering, but Ginny eventually decided to have melon followed by fillet steak cooked in wine with button mushrooms and tiny onions, and when the waiter came, Tony casually told him he would have the same, which disappointed her rather, but she told herself Toby must eat out in restaurants so often that choosing food no longer had the same enjoyment.

It was fun to sit and sip her sherry and look round the bar at all the other people, speculating on their identities and their reasons for being there. The young, pretty girl in the Laura Ashley print was clearly having a family birthday party, and there were a couple of obvious wedding anniversaries, as well as a good sprinkling of lovers, both of the married and unmarried variety, thought Ginny, feeling suddenly very worldly wise.

"What are you thinking?" Toby asked.

She gave a quick smile. "Oh, about all the other people who are here, wondering about what they're celebrating and if they're wondering about us."

He raised his eyebrows. "Why ever should they be?"

"No reason." She felt foolish suddenly. "I suppose I just like observing people. I always have."

"You and Max have more in common than you think." His voice sounded flat, almost bored, and Ginny flinched a little.

"I don't think so," she said stiltedly.

"Did he give you a hard time because you were coming out with me this evening?"

"Not really." Ginny shook her head. "But then why should he? It's none of his business where I go and what I do."

His smile was cynical. "Brave words, Ginny my sweet, but you should know by now as well as I do that Max has a habit of making things his business."

"But I'm not among them," she said quickly. "Can't we change the subject, please?"

"Of course." He paused for a moment. "Why don't you tell me about you, Ginny?"

"I'm not very interesting," she protested. "Besides, you know it already."

"I know very little about you. I know that you're domesticated, that you're a good cook, that you have a strong sense of family responsibility."

She pulled a slight face. "You make me sound very prim and—goody-goody. Is that how you see me?"

"Of course not. I think—" Toby hesitated.

"Yes?" she prompted.

"I think you're very sweet," he said lightly. "You're very different from the rest of the family, aren't you?"

"I suppose so," she said rather wryly. "Barbie was always the beauty and Tim's certainly the brains, if only he would use them more often. I was always just—Mouse. But I didn't mind," she added hurriedly.

"Mouse?" He smiled. "It suits you. Town mouse into country mouse. That didn't work terribly well, if I remember my Beatrix Potter."

"It has to work," she said. "For all our sakes."

"But what about your own sake? What do you want from life?"

Suddenly shy, she avoided his glance. "The usual things, I suppose," she mumbled.

"A husband, a home and security for the rest of your life?" He grimaced a little. "Could be a tall order, little Ginny, especially with a ready-made family in tow."

There was a silence. Was he warning her, she wondered miserably, that he wasn't good husband material? Had she been so obvious?

Pride came to her rescue, and she shrugged. "I wasn't really thinking in those terms. I—I haven't even been in love yet. Can't—can't I sow some wild oats before I settle down for ever to my domesticity?''

Toby looked amused. ''If that's what you want, my sweet, I expect it can be arranged.''

The waiter arrived at that moment to tell them that their table was ready. Toby took her hand as they stood up and Ginny felt her heart sing with happiness.

Facing him across the intimacy of the candlelit table in a corner of the cosy dining room, she began to feel shy again, wishing she had not issued quite such a blatant invitation, but he seemed unaware of her silence, chatting away easily about the new job he was hoping to get, designing the sets for a television soap opera still in the planning stage. Gradually she was able to relax and enjoy the food and wine when it was served.

It was lovely to sit down to a meal she had not prepared, and know that she would not be expected to clear away afterwards. She told Toby so, and he laughed.

''Poor Ginny, you sound like Cinderella! Will your lovely dress turn back into tatty jeans and a sweater on the stroke of midnight?''

She gave a mock shudder. ''I hope not!'' But she suffered a slight pang all the same. So Toby had regarded her ordinary appearance as tatty.

The waiter was hovering, offering more coffee, more liqueurs, but Ginny refused. She had already drunk more than she was accustomed to, and there had been wine in the food as well. Her head swam slightly as she stood up, and Toby took her arm.

''Home time, I think.'' He steered her between the tables towards the door. They were almost there when Ginny realised she was being closely scrutinised by someone. She turned slightly and met the unsmiling gaze of Vivien Lanyon as it deepened into a kind of incredulous recognition. Ginny sent her a dazzling smile, and received a small hostile nod in return. It was clear her metamorphosis had not been welcomed by her employer, and Ginny recalled with a sudden plunge of her spirits that it had been her sheer ordi-

nariness which had been her main recommendation to Mrs.
Lanyon in the first place. She was too taken up with her
digressing thoughts to pay much attention to where she was
going, and the next thing she knew she had collided with
one of the waiters who was leaning across a table pouring
wine. His arm jerked and a stream of wine shot across the
table.

"Oh!" Ginny was aghast. "I'm sorry. Look what I've
done!" she appealed to Toby, who no longer looked quite
so amused.

"It doesn't matter," he said briefly. "Come away, Ginny, before you do any more damage. The waiter will see to
it—that's what he's paid for."

Humiliated, she went ahead of him up the steps which
led to the double glass doors into the dining room. At the
door she glanced back, and saw Vivien Lanyon turn to one
of her table companions, a derisive smile playing about her
lips. Ginny's cheeks flamed. Of all the stupid things to do,
she berated herself silently as they emerged into the car
park. One clumsy act, and the glitter had gone from her
wonderful shining evening.

In the car, she tried again. "Toby, I'm so sorry about
what happened."

"Forget it," he advised briefly, leaning forward to flick
on the radio.

"But I should at least have offered to pay for more wine
for those people."

"At those prices? Don't be an idiot, Ginny. These things
happen and restaurants are prepared for it. I should have
realised you weren't used to alcohol."

She was mortified. Was that what he thought? Was that
what they had all thought? Even if she explained that it had
been seeing Mrs. Lanyon so unexpectedly which had caused
her momentary aberration, it would only sound like an excuse. It was probably better to do as he suggested, and try and
forget it had happened.

As they drove through the dark lanes, she began to relax
again. Toby seemed to have recovered his former good

temper, humming to the music, and after a while she joined in as well. Almost before she knew it, they were turning into the courtyard at Monk's Dower.

"It's funny, isn't it?" She was speaking her thoughts aloud. "Homeward journeys always seem faster than outward ones."

"Can't say I'd noticed." He switched off the engine and leaned back in his seat.

Her heart was hammering so loudly she thought that he must hear it. She tried to speak casually.

"I've had a wonderful time, Toby. Thank you."

"It was my pleasure. We must do it again some time," he returned.

She moistened her lips with the tip of her tongue. "Well— goodnight."

Toby got out of the driving seat and came round to open the passenger door for her. Ginny climbed out, and stood waiting, hoping that he would take her in his arms.

He gave a slight shiver. "In with you, my child. Your aunt was right about that frost, I think."

She said, "Yes," but her voice was almost inaudible. She walked away from him, her hands searching her bag automatically for her key. Behind her she heard the slam of his door and the sound of the car starting up. She made herself turn and, smiling brightly, return his wave as he drove off. Then she closed the door very carefully behind her, and burst into tears.

CHAPTER SEVEN

THE house was in darkness around her as she wept. Aunt Mary must have decided to have an early night, she thought, as she sat by the kitchen table, crumpling her wet handkerchief into a ball. And Barbie, of course, wouldn't be home yet, or at least there had been no sign of Max's car.

She was glad that she didn't have to face anyone. It wasn't at all the homecoming she had dreamed of. She'd imagined that Toby would accompany her into the house. That she would have made them both coffee—that they would have sat by the sitting-room fire drinking it until at last he put the cup aside and drew her very gently towards him.... And there her fantasy had petered out.

She stifled a sob. Instead she too was faced with the prospect of an early night, and she would have Barbie's questions to answer when her sister returned. How could she explain away the fact that she'd been deposited like an unwanted parcel in a left-luggage office? The metaphor made her smile in spite of herself.

No, she didn't want to go to bed, because she knew she would be unable to sleep. But nor did she want to be found sitting forlornly in the kitchen when Max returned with Barbie.

She reached up and began listlessly taking the pins out of her hair, shaking it loose around her face. Everything back to normal, she told herself drearily, combing it with her fingers. The dress and all that went with it had only been a façade after all. Underneath she was still Mouse.

She felt more tears well up and resolutely dammed them back. What she needed, she thought, was something to take her mind off what had just transpired. She glanced at her watch. It would probably be at least an hour before Max returned. She could go through to the study and so some more work. It wasn't what she wanted, but it would occupy her, and save her from useless recriminations. And she would see the headlights from Max's car and be able to slip back quietly to her own part of the house without anyone being any the wiser, she thought. She could pretend, perhaps, she had just returned herself.

She drew the study curtains before switching on the desk lamp, and settling down to work with fierce concentration. Eventually the words she was typing took over, and she began to live with the protagonists in Max's play, their troubles becoming more real to her than her own. She was almost sorry when she realised she had caught up with him again, and that there was no new material for her to transcribe.

She sighed as she collated her sheets and clipped them together. He was a superb writer, she thought wistfully. His work showed both humour and compassion. If she had just been given a copy of the play to read, she would have marked its author as a man she would want to meet, to know, to have as her friend, even as her lover. . . .

She put the sheets down on the desk with hands which shook, telling herself that she was becoming lightheaded. Perhaps Toby had been right all along, and she had had too much to drink.

But at the same time she knew this was why her fantasy of herself alone in the firelight with Toby never led to the obvious conclusion. Because if she let herself dream further, it was Max's arms which held her, and his mouth which explored hers with demanding urgency. Of course there was a rational explanation for that. He was the only man who had ever kissed her in passion, even if his predominating emotion had been anger. But she had wanted— needed Toby's kiss, Toby's caress to wipe that other disturbing image from her mind.

Because Max was not the kind of man she could ever

allow herself to dream about. He wasn't humorous or compassionate, she told herself vehemently. Because of him a girl had tried to kill herself—a girl who had loved him, and whom he had used. That was the fate awaiting those unwise enough to love the Max Hendricks of this world, and she could not, must not let it happen to her.

She gasped helplessly, as she realised where her thoughts were leading her. Love, she thought. *Love* in connection with Max Hendrick and herself. It was ludicrous, unthinkable. She hated him. It was Toby she was falling in love with.

It has to be Toby, she told herself raggedly. It just has to be.

The slam of the front door brought her to her feet in panic, fumbling for the lamp switch. She pulled aside the curtain and peeped out. Max's car was still missing from the courtyard, but that could be because he had put it away earlier in the garage in the old stable.

There was no doubt that it was his footsteps which she could hear coming down the hall. She tensed as they drew level with the study door, then relaxed as he went past with no alteration in his stride. At least he didn't know she was there. Probably he'd gone to the kitchen to make himself a hot drink, and she could escape back to her own part of the house while he was so engaged, and evade awkward explanations or any other kind of confrontation.

She stole to the door and listened for a long moment for signs of life beyond it before opening it and stepping out into the hall.

A stifled scream rose in her throat as a hand descended on her bare arm.

"So it is you," Max remarked pleasantly. His eyes went past her to the desk, the uncovered typewriter, and the pile of completed typescript.

"How much are you planning to charge me for this unsolicited overtime?" he enquired.

"Nothing at all," Ginny denied hotly. "I—I just felt like getting on with some work, that's all."

"I see." The dark eyes measured her, missing nothing, she thought almost hysterically, from her bedraggled finery to the tearstains on her cheeks. "What went wrong Ginevra?"

"Nothing at all," she denied defensively, trying to push past him. "I—I had a wonderful time. I just didn't want to go to bed straight away and...."

"Don't lie to me." He detained her easily, without exerting any particular pressure. "When a girl has been wined and dined, she doesn't usually come back and apply her nose to the grindstone without drawing breath—not without good reason, that is."

She said nothing, staring down at the floor until she thought she could have drawn from memory every knothole, every grain in the plank.

"Well?" he prompted, and the floor blurred and broke into a thousand shimmering pieces.

He said, "Oh, my God."

The next thing Ginny knew she was being deposited none too gently on the sofa in the drawing room while he kicked the reluctant fire into renewed life, adding extra wood from the box. She wanted to stop crying. She pressed her fists childishly against her eyes as if she would dam the tears back by sheer force, but they continued to fall down her pale cheeks.

"Drink this." Max was standing in front of her holding out a glass.

"What is it?" She accepted it gingerly.

"An accepted stimulant. Don't ask questions. Just drink."

It was like liquid fire in her throat and she grimaced. "I don't like it. It's like medicine."

His brows lifted. "You should speak of good cognac with more respect, my child."

"That's it, isn't it?" she said drearily, looking past him at the flames which were beginning to curl round the logs. "That sums it up. I didn't know this was cognac. I didn't know half the things on the menu tonight. I made an utter fool of myself on the way out of the restaurant. Toby called me a child as well.''

"Did he now?" There was a grim note in his voice.

"Oh, yes." She looked up at him. "And he was quite right. That's probably why...." She hesitated.

"Yes?"

"Probably why he didn't kiss me." She took another sip of the cognac. "I thought he would, you see. I wanted him to. But he didn't. End of story. Except this is what's made me realise...."

The cushions beneath her felt as soft as clouds, and she was floating away on them. She felt the glass taken from her hand and she looked up with a start. Max was standing looking down at her, a bleakness in his eyes which made her shrink back.

"What has all this made you realise, Ginevra?"

"That I really was a child, I suppose. Because if I'd been older in my ways, more sophisticated, I could have made him see I wanted him to kiss me. Couldn't I?"

"Probably." He was very still.

She said almost dreamily, "Barbie would have known how to do it. She told me years ago that men always know when girls are—available. It's a sort of chemistry. And I haven't got it."

He said almost conversationally, "What bloody rubbish you talk sometimes, Ginevra. Just because my singularly insensitive cousin didn't bestow the statutory goodnight peck, it doesn't make you any less desirable."

"No?" she said. "But you kissed Barbie, didn't you? Not because it meant anything, perhaps, but because she was beautiful and—and desirable—and *there*. Well, I was there too, but he didn't touch me. Perhaps I just give out the wrong vibrations." She gave a little unhappy laugh. "Barbie told me I was the worst case of arrested virginity she'd ever seen. Maybe she's right."

"And maybe she isn't." There was anger in his voice. "You're not very lucky, are you, Ginevra, either in your relations or your men? And there's nothing wrong with your vibrations, believe me."

"Isn't there?" She looked at him bleakly. "You kissed me once, but it wasn't because you—desired me. It was because you were angry, and you wanted to punish me."

His lips twisted. "If you believe that, Ginevra, then you really are a child. You're both attractive and desirable, whatever alternative impression the events of the past few hours may have given you. Any man with blood in his veins would want you."

She said in a very low voice, "Do you want me, Max?" Panic assailed her as soon as the words were uttered. This was madness, or at the very least bravado, inspired by the wine she had drunk at dinner. I must go, she thought, trying to lever herself up from the cushions. I've got to get out of here.

But she was too late. He was beside her, one long arm reaching for her, drawing her swiftly and inexorably against him.

"Yes, I want you." His voice sounded harsh to her frightened ears. "Shall I prove it?"

She was rigid in his embrace, dry-mouthed, not knowing what to expect, scared of what she herself had invited.

"Relax," he murmured, his mouth so close to her cheek that she could feel the warmth of his breath on her skin, then he began to kiss her very gently, his lips trailing featherlight along her cheekbone and down, teasingly, to the lobe of her ear. It was gentle and not at all alarming, and she began to relax against the unfamiliar warmth and hardness of his body, eyes closed, while he continued to explore her face very softly with his lips.

She had thought his mouth hard, she told herself incredulously, but it was nothing of the sort. It was warm and firm and infinitely pleasurable. Dangerously so, said a small warning voice in the back of her mind.

He kissed her eyes and her hair and her cheeks, and her throat where her pulse was behaving most erratically, and eventually, inevitably she turned her head slightly, offering him her mouth with total candour.

Max moved a little, slipping one arm down under her knees and lifting her slender body even closer, so that she lay across him.

Then he kissed her mouth, parting her lips quite ruthlessly, making no further concessions to her innocence. She felt as helpless as a doll in his arms. A rag doll, she thought, soft and limp-limbed, unable to think, unable to move of its own volition.

Her hands crept up over his shoulders, discovering their lean muscularity. Max's shirt felt smooth and silken and expensive under her fingers and she found herself wondering how his skin would feel, and again that tiny warning sounded in her brain, so that this time she pulled herself away with a little gasp.

"What's the matter?" Max stared down at her. In the firelight his face had an oddly bitter brooding look. "Have you suddenly thought better of your little experiment? Well, don't get agitated, darling. Just close your eyes and pretend it's Toby, and that will make everything all right."

This time his mouth was almost brutal in its possession and she should have been frightened, she should have been repelled, only she wasn't. She felt faintly bewildered, that was all, bewildered that he could think she was capable of imagining that it was Toby who held her. Toby who was kissing her as if he would drain the last drop of sweetness from her mouth. The time for imagining was long past, she knew that now, and this was reality—that very reality she had feared to face for so long. No pretense in the world could disguise the fact that it was Max's arms in which she lay—Max who was slowly but mercilessly awakening her to the realisation of her own sensuality.

She whimpered in her throat as his kiss deepened, her fingers twining restlessly in his dark hair. He was holding her so closely that she felt as if at any moment her body might melt into his, to merge and blend for all eternity.

His hand caressed her throat, then moved downwards, his fingers warm and languorous on her bare shoulder, tangling in the bow which fastened her dress. His mouth gentled, and little sensuous tremors pulsated through her body, as if she sensed the more intimate demand he was making of her. And then the bow slipped loose, and the dress fell away, baring the slight curve of one rose-tipped breast.

She heard Max catch his breath sharply, then his hand slid down to cup and caress, and a slow sweet shiver ran through her as if all her life she had been waiting for just this moment and just his touch on her body, and she wanted more, much more, she thought, as her head fell back against his shoulder and her body arched blindly, sweetly towards his in surrender.

Only there was no surrender. Max gave a swift, muffled curse, and pushed her away almost to arm's length, so that she collapsed back against the sofa cushions again, her eyes wide with alarm.

He rose and went over to the fireplace, reaching for the pack of cheroots and lighter on the mantlepiece.

"It's time you went home, Ginny," he said, and his voice was totally expressionless.

"But why?" she faltered. "Is something the matter? Did I do something wrong?"

He laughed, but there was no amusement in the sound. "No, darling, nothing at all. You were very responsive and very sweet. Toby should be in for a delightful surprise at your next encounter with him."

His words stung, and she felt the colour storming into her face. She sat up, pulling the bodice of her dress up to cover herself, her fingers fumbling as she retied the bow. "What do you mean?"

"Oh, come now, Ginerva." He drew deeply on the cheroot, his dark face set in harsh lines as he regarded her. "That was what it was all about, wasn't it? A little sip at the cup of knowledge to see if the taste appealed to you—which it clearly does. But the lesson in love ends there, my sweet." He saw her uncomprehending look, and his mouth twisted cynically. "The next lesson takes place in bed, darling, and while I'm ready and more than willing to continue your education, I doubt if it's what you want. Besides," his voice hardened, "Toby would care for my leavings as little as I'd care for his."

For a moment Ginny was stunned into silence. Was that what he thought—that she'd been using him as a substitute for his cousin? Rage and humiliation welled up in her.

"How—how dare you!" She got to her feet. "I wouldn't ...I mean I wouldn't have allowed...you flatter yourself...."

"You'd have had very little choice in the matter. I'd have seen to that," Max said flatly. "Just be thankful I'm not inclined to take advantage of you, and don't push your luck where I'm concerned again."

"How very chivalrous of you!" Her voice shook. "I'd be very impressed, probably, if I didn't know your real motivation. You're terrified of another Laura episode, aren't you?"

For a moment he stared at her, then with a muttered expletive he threw his cheroot into the flames.

"How the hell did you find out about that? Oh, don't tell me. Cousin Toby strikes again. I always did underestimate that bastard."

"He told me in order to warn me—because he thought you'd probably make a pass at me and...."

"Is that how you describe tonight's little episode?" His voice was derisive. "You were making all the running, sweetheart, or had you forgotten?"

Her hands were clenched so tightly into fists at her sides that the knuckles showed white. "Is that your excuse for what happened to Laura? Did she make all the running too?"

The expression on his face frightened her. He took a step towards her and she instinctively retreated, stumbling against the sofa as she did so. He stood, his hands resting on his hips, watching contemptuously as she struggled to regain her balance.

"You'd better go, Ginevra. You accused me tonight of making love to you once in order to punish you. As God's my witness, that's nothing to what I'll do to you if I get my hands on you again. Now get out of my sight."

From the comparative safety of the doorway, she hurled her last bolt.

"You—you use everyone. You don't even see women as people. You're despicable!"

"Am I?" The frightening anger seemed to have died down suddenly, and there was a great weariness in his voice. "Yet only this evening I could have had your sister, Ginevra, and a few minutes ago, in spite of all your virtuous protests, I could have had you. If I was the kind of mindless lecher you suggest, I'd hardly be spending the rest of the night alone. Now go to bed, and be thankful that it's your own bed you're going to."

Ginny was still trembling when she reached her room. She shut the door and leaned against the panels for a moment, trying to steady her ragged breathing.

"Is that you at last?" Barbie's voice came petulantly from the darkness. The light clicked on with dazzling suddenness, and she stared resentfully across the room at her sister. "I needn't ask if you've had a good time, I suppose?" she added, studying Ginny's dishevelled appearance.

Ginny pressed her hands to her burning cheeks. "Yes, thank you." Her voice sounded prim and stilted even to her own ears, and Barbie laughed unkindly.

"You look as if you've been dragged through a hedge backwards," she observed. "I hope you didn't allow your ardent lover to tear that dress."

"No." Ginny removed it with exaggerated care and placed it on a hanger. Her sister lay back against the pillow watching her.

"You must have developed hidden depths, Mouse," she said at last as Ginny climbed into bed. "To be honest, I thought your evening would probably be a yawn a minute, and you'd be safely home by closing time."

Ginny switched off the bedside lamp and turned on to her stomach, burying her face in the pillow. Lying in the darkness, she wished, not for the first time in her life, that Barbie had been different—the sort of person she could have confided in. As it was, it was much better to let her think she'd been involved in some heavy petting session with Toby rather than the truth.

She wished desperately that she had her room to herself as well, so that she could cry herself to sleep.

There was only one consolation in the catalogue of disasters she kept reciting to herself during the sleepless hours which followed. At least Max was convinced that it was still Toby she wanted. There was no way that he could guess the hideous, shaming truth that, in spite of everything that had happened between them, she had fallen deeply and desperately in love with him.

SHE felt depressed and jaded the next morning. She had to force herself to get out of bed and dress herself in a pair of the jeans and one of the elderly sweaters which had aroused Toby's derision. She grimaced at herself as she dragged a comb through her hair before confining it carelessly at the nape of her neck with an elastic band.

Aunt Mary's glance was disapproving as she entered the kitchen. "Did you oversleep, my dear?"

Ginny forced a smile. "I suppose I must have."

"You'd better hurry with your breakfast if you're going to be on time for work." Aunt Mary produced a plate of bacon and eggs from the hot cupboard and brought it to the table. Ginny looked down at the food with a sinking heart. All she had planned on having was a cup of strong black coffee, but she managed a grateful murmur, and began to struggle with her breakfast forkful by forkful.

"Did you return home very late last night?" Aunt Mary seated herself at the table and poured another cup of tea from the pot.

"Quite late," Ginny said cautiously.

"How strange." Aunt Mary stirred the tea reflectively. "I thought I heard Toby's car outside before I put my light out. I must have been mistaken."

"Yes." Ginny ate a tiny sliver of bacon. For a moment she was sorely tempted to fling herself into her great-aunt's arms and confess the whole sorry mess, but that would be a selfish act, she knew. Aunt Mary had been looking frail lately, and Ginny had no wish to burden her with unnecessary worries. Besides, she was under no illusion as to what Aunt Mary would say about her conduct. Now, in the cold light of day, she could hardly believe it herself.

"Did you have a pleasant evening?" Aunt Mary was enquiring.

"It was very nice. The food was superb." That was safe ground, Ginny thought, embarking on an enthusiastic survey of the menu. "The wine was lovely too," she added rather lamely as her recital closed. Too lovely, an ironic inner voice reminded her.

"And how was dear Toby? Will you be seeing him today?"

"I'm not quite sure." Ginny crossed her fingers below the table.

Aunt Mary nodded. "I'm glad you enjoyed yourself, my dear. I've often thought how little enjoyment there is for a girl of your age tied to this kind of job in the country. It's right that you should be able to lay your burdens and responsibilities down occasionally."

"I really don't look at my life in that way." Ginny pushed her plate to one side.

"And if you did, I would probably be the last person you would admit it to," said Aunt Mary with a short sigh. "Oh, my dear, how I wish there was someone who would take the pressure from you—share the burden with you. At one time I hoped...." She paused, as if aware she was saying too much. "But I suppose I was just being foolish."

She means Toby, Ginny thought wryly. She said gently, "There's no question of that, Aunt Mary."

"No." Her great-aunt sighed again. "And I really did think...." She shrugged and gave a faint smile. "One of the perils of being an old maid, I suppose. An overdeveloped sense of romanticism." She glanced at her watch and exclaimed in dismay. "And here I am keeping you chatting over my nonsense when you should have been at work several minutes ago! Max will be wondering where you are."

"I doubt that," Ginny said under her breath as she dumped her used plate in the sink. "I doubt that very much."

It took nearly all the courage of which she was capable to go through the dividing door, and along the passage to the study. Max was on the telephone when she entered, and he did not look up or acknowledge her presence in any way. She did not go to her seat but stood in front of his desk, waiting quietly, once, unobtrusively wiping her damp palms on her jeans, until he said a "Goodbye" and replaced his receiver. His eyes were as cold as winter as they met hers.

She said hurriedly, "I've come to apologize—for last night." She paused, but he said nothing, nor was his expression particularly encouraging. Ginny swallowed and went on, "It must have been the wine—I'm just not used to it." Still silence, so she added rather defensively, "And then you gave me that brandy...."

Max raised his eyebrows. "This is beginning to sound more like another accusation than an apology."

"I didn't mean it like that," she protested. "I—I just didn't want you to think—to get the wrong impression. I know how badly I behaved, and I'm sorry...." Her voice trailed away.

"Now that I can believe," he said sardonically. "It's a condition known as hating yourself in the morning. So what are you expecting from me, Ginevra? A similar display of penitence? You'll be disappointed, I'm afraid. My sole regret is that I didn't finish what you began—drunk or sober."

She flushed. "You—You're not making this very easy for me...."

"Do you really expect me to?" he countered derisively. "You were let off the hook last night, darling, and don't you forget it."

"I'm not likely to forget anything," she said wretchedly. "Do you want me to hand in my notice?"

"No," he said, and her heart lifted slightly, only to sink

again at his next words. "It wouldn't be particularly convenient at this stage to have to get used to another typist."

But when the play is finished, she thought miserably as she went to her own desk, what then?

Halfway through the morning Vivien Lanyon arrived, walking into the study unannounced.

"Max darling!" She walked round the desk as he rose to greet her, and lifted her cheek for his kiss. "You hadn't forgotten that we're lunching with the Craigs?"

"No, I hadn't forgotten," he said. "Give me five minutes, and I'll be with you."

When he had gone, Mrs. Lanyon sank down on to his chair, producing cigarettes and a lighter from her bag. Her eyes flicked disdainfully over Ginny.

"Quite a metamorphosis," she drawled. "Tell me, do you really think it appropriate for someone in your position to be seen around the local night-spots with Max's cousin?"

"Perhaps the person you should really ask is Max's cousin," said Ginny, stung. "And I thought the feudal system had died out centuries ago."

Vivien Lanyon lifted an eyebrow and gave a light laugh. "My dear child, that isn't what I meant at all. But surely you must have realised by now that Max's cousin is—*persona non grata* at Monk's Dower. I should have thought as you work for him that Max's wishes might carry some weight with you, but obviously not."

She swung around on the chair and stared through the window. Everything about her spoke of being handmade, expensive and chic, and Ginny felt a wave of what could only be jealousy well up inside her. She found herself wondering a little bitterly what Mrs. Lanyon would say if she told her the truth—that if Max summoned her from the world's end, she would go to him. But what use was there even thinking in those terms? For her, the realisation that what she had felt for Toby was only the merest shadow of desire had come too late. And it changed nothing. Max was still the same person he had always been, and so was she.

And she was learning the hard way that sometimes you loved someone in spite of what they were, and not because of it.

Lying awake and miserable the previous night, she had acknowledged to herself how desperately she had fought against her initial unwilling attraction to him, how she had counted on Toby to rescue her from the consequences of her own folly. A ridiculous scheme, as she now admitted, trying to fight her feelings for one man by artifically creating another relationship in her mind. Because that was all it had been with Toby. He had been kind to her at first, probably because it suited him, she thought, and she had been attracted because he was indeed attractive and she was lonely. But anything more had been her own invention, a protective shell to hide her true emotions from the world, and even from herself.

Her eyes went instinctively to the door as it swung open again, and Max came in, shrugging his arms into his car coat. For a brief, unguarded moment, Ginny let herself drink in all the lean length of him, remembering all too vividly the touch of his body against hers. As he turned abruptly towards her, she had to look away hurriedly, scared that he would see the naked hunger in her eyes.

He said, "I'm not sure when I'll be back, Ginevra, so when you've finished what you're doing, you can have the rest of the day off. Get some rest. You look as if you need it."

Vivien Lanyon gave vent to that same silvery laugh. "I should think she does need it, darling, or am I telling tales out of school? Your little secretary bird was flying high last night, and probably has a king-sized hangover to remember it by."

"Indeed?" Max's face was stony.

Vivien Lanyon stood up, smoothing down her skirt. "I've been trying to give her some good advice, but she doesn't seem terribly grateful. These children never realise; how foolish they make themselves look when they drink more than they're used to, and in poor Miss Clayton's case it seemed to go straight to her legs.'' She gave a little reminiscent smile. ''I'd allow a decent interval to elapse before you visit Les Deux Etrangers again, if I were you, and in the meantime learn to be a little less gauche, perhaps.''

As she swept out of the room, her perfume seemed to hang on the air like the scent of some malignant flower.

Ginny sat there too crushed to move. She heard the car drive away and then she got up very slowly as if movement hurt her, and went over to the window. The courtyard was empty and she was empty too, she thought, turning away and moving across to the door.

As she went through the dividing door, she met Aunt Mary looking faintly worried.

''Did you say that Barbara could take the car, Ginevra?''

''Why, no. The subject never came up.''

Aunt Mary sighed. ''I thought not!'' she exclaimed. ''Well, she went off in it over an hour ago with no word to say when she would be coming back. And I only hope that she's taken Muffin with her, because I can't find him anywhere.''

''That's hardly likely,'' said Ginny, startled. Barbie had never displayed much interest in the dog, even in the old days, and she had ignored him completely since her arrival. ''Oh, Aunt Mary, you don't think she just let him out, do you? Not after we've been so careful. I'll have to go and look for him.''

''But how can you? What will Max say?''

Ginny bit her lip. ''Max isn't around to say anything. He's gone to have lunch with some people called Craig, taking Mrs. Lanyon with him. I have the rest of the day off.''

She found Muffin's lead and set off, not really knowing which direction to take. There was no accounting for the distance a really determined dog could cover in an hour's illicit freedom. She supposed she should have emphasized to her sister that Muffin wasn't really allowed to run free here, but she was forced to admit she had been too much absorbed in her own affairs to think of such mundane matters.

She walked, and called and whistled, listening for the sound of excited barking, however distant, but there was nothing. She was tired and growing hoarse by the time she arrived at the Manor. The first person she saw was Kathy crossing the stable yard.

"Hello, stranger." The older woman looked her up and down, smiling. "What brings you here?"

Ginny led out the dog lead mutely, and Kathy groaned. "Run off again, has he? Well, I hope for your sake he hasn't got into any mischief. Mr. Henderson was over here only the other day playing war about rogue dogs. Reckoned he'd caught a couple in among his young lambs."

"Not Muffin," Ginny protested. "It couldn't have been. We've been so careful."

"I don't think it would matter what dog it was, if Mr. Henderson got hold of it. Stock's valuable, you know."

Ginny said again with a small note of desperation in her voice, "But it couldn't have been Muffin! It mustn't be him. I don't know what Tim would do if—if anything happened to Muffin." She flexed her shoulders wearily. "I think I must have walked in a complete circle, and there's no sign of him anywhere."

"Been walking, have you? What's happened to that old car of yours? Broken down?"

"No," Ginny sighed. "My sister borrowed it."

"Well, you don't want to be out too long, not without a proper coat," Kathy said censoriously. "There's rain on the way. I'd run you back myself, only I have to wait here for a couple of phone calls." She winked. "I don't suppose they're that important, really, but they would be if I missed them."

Ginny gave a stilted little smile. "Oh yes, Mrs. Lanyon's out to lunch, isn't she?" She hoped her tone was casual enough.

Kathy chuckled. "Taking her future husband on a tour of the neighbourhood. It's the Craigs today. He's the local M.F.H. and she's a magistrate. What your boss will make of them, heaven knows, though they're nice enough in their way. Perhaps they'll persuade Mr. Hendrick to join the Hunt. He hasn't shown a great deal of interest, even though he's such a good rider."

Ginny wanted to say something flip like, "How odd, when he's a born predator." But she couldn't. The pain deep inside her at Kathy's laughing words was too sharp and too real.

Eventually she said in a low voice, "Do—do you know when the engagement will be announced?"

"I'd have thought you'd have been the first to know that," Kathy said cheerfully. "As you're working for him, I daresay you'll be called on to put the announcement in *The Times.* It'll make a bit of a stir locally too. It's been an open secret for years now how hard up she is, and he's certainly not short of money."

"No," said Ginny, remembering what Toby had told her about Max inheriting wealth from his parents. She was glad to be able to make the excuse that she must continue her search, and escape from the environs of the Manor, and all its associations. She thrust her hands into the pockets of her jacket and trudged along, too despondent even to look into the fields she was passing for the missing Muffin. It was shattering to learn that Max's marriage to Vivien Lanyon was so confidently expected in the locality, yet she supposed that logically it made a lot of sense. He would be getting an attractive, sophisticated woman with an established social position in return for the money he would be expected to plough into the estate, and he would be acquiring the Manor as well, a far grander and more impressive residence than Monk's Dower.

A line of poetry recalled from her schooldays surfaced in her mind. *"There never was a better bargain driven."* And yet that wasn't entirely appropriate, she thought desolately, because wasn't the bargain referred to the fact that *"My true love hath my heart and I have his"*?

She dug her teeth into her lower lip. Phrases like "true love" might have rung true in Elizabethan times, but not now. Not any more. These days you might admit to "fancying" someone, but that was all. You simply found someone else, and if the pain inside you said that there would never be anyone else—that you'd met the man who filled your heart and your world to the exclusion of everyone else, then you certainly didn't confess it—even to yourself, she thought unhappily.

That was the path to almost certain misery, down which she had already trodden much too far. And the pretense that would be required of her would be even worse. She would have to smile, mouth conventional good wishes, maybe even send announcements to newspapers as Kathy had predicted, and all the time she would have to hide that she was slowly bleeding to death inside herself.

She shivered slightly as the first raindrops struck her, casting an apprehensive glance at the sky where clouds were piling in from the west, blotting out the hopeful sun. The thin corduroy jacket she had thrown on earlier was certainly not going to be adequate in the downpour which was threatening.

Aunt Mary would be getting worried too, she thought ruefully, glancing at her watch. She'd been missing for a couple of hours already, and she still had to make her way back to Monk's Dower through the lanes. She groaned inwardly as she turned up her coat collar. It would take her at least half an hour to walk home and she would be drenched. She would have to wait until Barbie came back with the car, and then search again before it got too dark, she thought.

Twenty minutes later, the idea of any activity other than soaking in a hot bath was becoming totally unacceptable. Her wet jeans were sticking clammily to her legs, and her shoes were squelching as she picked her way along. Her hair was sopping too, and cold droplets ran down her neck beneath the collar of her sweater.

When she heard the sound of a car engine coming up behind her in the narrow lane, she squeezed herself as close to the hedge as possible and waited. She had had one drenching already from a tractor which had roared past without its driver even seeming to see her. At least this car didn't seem to be going too fast, she thought thankfully. She turned to look in its direction, wiping her eyes, and her heart gave a painful twist. She looked round wildly, longing for a friendly gate she could dart through into some sort of sanctuary, but there was no shelter of any kind.

He had seen her, of course. She knew it was inevitable, even before the car passed her and stopped. Max got out and came towards her. His face was coldly furious, and his tone matched it as he said, "Trying to catch pneumonia, Ginevra?"

"No," she assured him through chattering teeth. "I came out in rather a hurry, you see. I didn't realise it was going to rain."

"Vivien's groom said you were looking for that damned dog of yours. Why in God's name didn't you bring your car? How far have you walked?"

"Miles," she said wearily. "It never occurred to me he'd be so hard to find. And Barbie borrowed the car. I suppose she assumed I'd be working this afternoon, and wouldn't need it."

"Your sister took the car?" There was an odd note in his voice that might have been anger. Ginny's heart sank. Barbie would not thank her for rousing Max's temper where she was concerned.

She said in a placatory tone, "I don't mind her taking the car, Max. It's very dull for her here, after all. There are at least shops in Market Harford she can look round."

He took her arm. "Get in the car."

"I can't," she protested, hanging back. "I'll drip all over your beautiful upholstery."

Max said something very rude and succinct about the car's upholstery, and she found herself being almost bundled into the passenger seat. She caught a brief, dismaying glimpse of herself in the driving mirror as she collapsed in a breathless heap, her hair hanging in rats' tails, her eyes enormous in her pale face.

He got in beside her and started the engine, flicking on

the heater as he did so. As the warmth began to penetrate her chilled bones, Ginny began almost perceptibly to relax. The murmur of the engine and the swish of the windshield wipers began to exercise an almost soporific effect, and she sat up straighter in her seat, fighting her tiredness. She stole a sideways glance at her companion, who was staring ahead of him, an enigmatic, almost brooding expression on his face.

She wondered with a little ache of her heart if he was thinking of the woman he had just left, and at that moment he turned his head slightly and their eyes met. She felt the colour creep into her face, and said hurriedly to cover her embarrassment, "I hope you enjoyed your lunch."

"It was very successful." His voice sounded laconic.

It was like pressing on a bad tooth, but she had to go on. "And Mrs.—Mrs. Lanyon. Did she enjoy it?"

"I think it fulfilled most of her expectations," he said smoothly. "You're very solicitous all of a sudden, Ginevra. It must be the onset of delirium. I'd better get you home as soon as possible."

Home, Ginny thought bitterly, as the car responded to his touch on the accelerator. What home was there for her at Monk's Dower with Vivien Lanyon, she was sure, looking for an excuse to be rid of her her?

As they turned into the courtyard, she saw a Land Rover standing in front of the house. She glanced at Max and saw his lip tighten. He said, "I think you've got trouble, Ginny."

His hand was firm on her arm as he helped her out. There was something lying in the back of the Land Rover, she noticed, as Max hurried her past, something covered by a piece of sacking, and then they were in the kitchen.

Aunt Mary was sitting at the kitchen table, looking pale and ill, and Tim was standing just in front of her, his face so white that his freckles stood out in contrast. There was a stranger here, wearing a mud-stained raincoat and wellingtons. He turned as they came in and Ginny saw a ruddy, weatherbeaten face that would normally have looked cheerful and good-natured, but was now grim.

He said, "You'll be Miss Clayton, I'm thinking. My name's Henderson."

Ginny parted her lips to speak, but before she could utter a word, Tim took a step forward.

He burst out, "He's shot him! This beastly man's shot Muffin—and he's dead...he's dead!"

The almost dazed expression on his face crumpled suddenly and shockingly into a misery too deep for words, then the tears came and he was a small, desperately upset boy looking for comfort. Ginny reached for him, but he went past her as if he hadn't seen her, and with a sense of shock she registered him clinging, sobbing to Max, and Max's arms closing protectively round him.

He said over Tim's head, "I suppose it was absolutely necessary."

"I'm afraid so, Mr. Hendrick. Two lambs dead, and the varmints after a third. After I'd shot your dog, the other one ran off, damn it. But I'll get him."

Max said, "Yes." Then, looking at Aunt Mary, "Miss Clayton, will you take Ginny upstairs and see she gets into some dry things as soon as possible? I'll take care of Tim and—see to things generally."

Ginny knew what he meant. She remembered the limp bundle in the back of the Land Rover, and her stomach lurched unsteadily. She could feel Aunt Mary's hand on her arm, but she was incapable of movement. She was watching Max with Tim, recognising a gentleness she had never realised existed before as he handled the child, quieting his sobs, calming him, making him turn and face Mr. Henderson who was clearly becoming more upset and embarrassed with every moment that passed.

She thought in a kind of agony, "Oh, poor Tim. He's going to be so hurt when Max marries Vivien Lanyon and we have to leave here. So hurt."

And she knew that for all their sakes she had to get them away from Monk's Dower before they could be hurt any more.

CHAPTER EIGHT

It was a conviction she carried with her all during the next hectic hour while she obediently took the prescribed hot bath which Aunt Mary ran for her. It restored some of the warmth to her cold limbs, but it could not reach the deeper, icier chill in her heart.

Nothing, she thought drearily, as she shrugged herself into the comfort of her old dressing gown, except time and distance would dispel that. The length of time was beyond her control, but she could do something about the distance.

Aunt Mary was waiting in her bedroom. "I've turned down your bed, my dear. I think you should have a rest, and I'll bring you something warm to drink."

Ginny smiled a little wearily. The time was long gone, she thought, when she was a child to be cosseted and comforted with bed and hot drinks. She had situations to face, decisions to make.

"I must go downstairs, Aunt Mary," she said gently. "I must talk to Tim."

"Max is looking after him." Aunt Mary's tone indicated that she found this a more than satisfactory state of affairs. "You have nothing to worry about. He's taking care of everything."

"But we can't let him—surely you see that?" Ginny turned to her aunt, spreading out her hands in appeal. "He—he probably means to be kind, but...."

She faltered as she met her great-aunt's astonished glance. There was no way she would be able to make her understand, she thought. Aunt Mary's generation belonged to a time when male superiority and dominance had been unquestioned.

She tried again. "Max isn't part of our family. He—he's my employer, that's all. We can't involve him in our troubles."

"Are you sure he isn't involved already?" Aunt Mary asked.

"Quite sure." Ginny tried to make her voice firm. "He has his own life to lead, and we mustn't depend on him. It—it worried me to see Tim rush to him like that."

"I don't suppose it worried Max," Aunt Mary said drily. "He probably found it perfectly natural under the circumstances. Tim misses his father very much, you know."

"Yes, I know." The tears she had been struggling to control pricked at the back of Ginny's eyelids. "But all the same, he can't be allowed to turn Max into a kind of surrogate father."

"No," Aunt Mary agreed. "That would be most unsuitable, but I think Tim regards him more in the light of an elder brother."

Ginny bent her head. "I don't find that particularly suitable either," she said in a muffled voice.

When Aunt Mary had gone downstairs to fetch the hot drink, she towelled her hair, then found her hand-drier and plugged it in, brushing her hair free of tangles under the current of warm air.

Aunt Mary clearly had no premonitions about the uncertainty of their future at Monk's Dower, she thought unhappily. She even seemed to think that Max was prepared to take the role of man of the family on his shoulders, which under the circumstances was ironic to say the least. Perhaps she should have warned her great-aunt that Max would probably soon have a family of his own. And even if this had not been the case, there would have been Toby's casual warning about ready-made families to bring her back to reality.

The noise of the drier prevented her from hearing the door opening, and the first inkling she received that she was no longer alone was Max's hand on her shoulder. She recoiled with a little cry.

"Oh, for God's sake!" he said impatiently. "I'm neither a ghost nor a rapist, Ginevra. Your great-aunt asked me to bring you this soup. She says you're to drink it while it's hot."

She put the drier aside and took the proffered mug with a muttered word of thanks.

He sat down on the edge of the dressing table, watching her in silence. After a moment or two he said, "I'm sorry about your dog, Ginevra. Had you had him for a long time?"

"He was still quite a young dog, really," she said haltingly. "But he was just—part of our lives. Part of the old days." She heard her voice start to shake, and controlled it with an effort. "It's rather ironic, isn't it? I uprooted us all and brought us here for security, and safety, but it isn't working out at all that way. I thought I knew best, but what did I know?"

"The country can often be as much of a jungle as any town," said Max. "But you can't blame yourself for what's happened today."

"I can and I do. Kathy—Mrs. Lanyon's groom—warned me. I should have taken more care. . . ."

"You took all the care you reasonably could. You can't be in two places at once. Nor can you hold yourself responsible for every disaster which happens. Get a sense of proportion, my child."

"I am responsible," she said in a low, fierce voice. "They're my family. They depend on me."

"And who do you depend on, Ginny? Yourself? That's a situation fraught with pitfalls, isn't it?"

"Perhaps." She cupped her hands round the mug and drank some of the soup. She wished with all her heart that he would go downstairs, away from her. It was disturbing to have him so close, and know that, just the same, there might have been a million miles between them.

"But you don't depend on your sister?" She saw him glance across at the other bed, still unmade and littered with discarded tights and other garments.

"She has her own life—her own responsibilities."

His mouth twisted. "I'd be interested to hear what they are some time." He gave the other bed a look of distaste. "Are you expected to act as her maid along with everything else?"

"Of course not," she denied quickly, closing her mind to the number of times in the past when she had made Barbie's bed and hung her clothes away. "She probably went out in rather a hurry today and forgot...." Her voice tailed away lamely as she encountered his sardonic gaze.

"Very loyal," he commented. "What a pity you aren't as ready to make excuses for me."

"You don't need me to defend you," she muttered.

"Or to accuse me either," he said drily. "But that doesn't stop you, Ginevra. You were very quick to fling the Laura Hertford episode in my face—or at least the version you'd heard of it. Would you like to hear my side of the story?"

"No. I—I've apologized for mentioning that. What you did—whatever happened is none of my my business." There was a note of desperation in her voice.

"Don't you think you may have made it your business?" He spoke evenly, but there was an underlying note of anger there.

"Please," she said, and her voice shook. "Can't we just forget everything that was said last night? I'm deeply ashamed. Isn't that enough for you?"

He said pleasantly, "You know bloody well it isn't."

He reached out and took the soup from her suddenly nerveless fingers, setting it down on the dressing table out of harm's way. Then he reached for her. For a moment Ginny was rigid, her head thrown back in silent protest, her fingers splayed against the hard wall of his chest, as she fought him with her mind as well as her body. But he lifted a hand and fastened it to her damp hair quite unhurriedly, allowing his other hand to slide the length of her body to her hip, and with a little moan she let herself surrender to the sensations that it seemed his slightest touch could engender in her.

He drew her towards him gently but inexorably until their bodies touched, trapping her between the hard muscles of his thighs, and then he was kissing her, his mouth moving on hers in sweet torment until her lips parted helplessly beneath his insistence.

Her last coherent thought told her that this was madness, and then she was swept away on the dark tide of delight sweeping through her body. Her own hands clung, touched, discovered. All her senses heightened in some strange way. The scent, the feel of him was all about her. Her mouth, her body seemed to breath him and in all the crazy swirling world he had created, he was the only reality.

The shabby old dressing gown was no barrier at all to his seeking hands. His caresses were gentle and without haste and as he touched her skin, she began to tremble. His mouth left hers and travelled slowly along her jawline and down the slender column of her throat, leaving a trail of featherlight kisses that ended only at the hollow between her breasts. Then the warmth of his lips was rediscovering the proof of her arousal which his hands had already ascertained, and she heard herself moan a little in pleasure, blind and deaf to everything except the clamour of her newly awakened instincts.

When his lips finally abandoned their slow, sweet adoration of her, she felt almost bereft, her hands going up to cradle his head and draw him down to her again, but with a groan of renunciation he put her away from him.

"Have some mercy on me, Ginny," he said huskily. "I can't take you now. This isn't the time or the place." He folded his arms about her, pulling her against him so closely that the fastenings on his clothing bit into her flesh. His lips sought the delicate hollow beneath her ear, and the hammering pulse at the base of her throat. He whispered against her skin, "Darling Ginny, flower girl, come to me tonight. Don't make me wait any longer."

His words seemed to hang in the silence which followed, and as she heard them and absorbed their meaning, all the warmth and emotion drained away out of her, leaving her cold and empty. She stepped away from him, her hands automatically pulling the sheltering folds of the dressing gown around her body, tightening its sash with fingers that shook.

Max said sharply and on a rising note of interrogation, "Ginny?" He lifted himself away from the edge of the dressing table and she took a step backwards.

"No!" Her voice was equally sharp. "No, don't touch me!"

His eyes met hers for one incredulous moment, then bewilderment faded, and she saw the more familiar sardonic look return. He raised his hands for a moment to look down at them, studying them as if they were something alien and unfamiliar which he had been asked to identify, then with a slight shrug he thrust them into the pockets of his jacket and sent her a glance of mocking challenge.

"So my touch is suddenly abhorrent to you once again, Ginevra," he drawled. "You should have told me before. I'd have sworn only a minute or two ago you couldn't have enough of it. In fact, I could draw a map of your body from memory."

His gaze seemed to strip her bare, and instinctively she hugged her arms across her breasts, drawing a soft laugh from him as she did so.

"It's a little late for that, my sweet," he mocked. "And I still have the taste of you. You can't cover or remove it from my reach. God," he added savagely, "I should have had every inch of you, and asked your permission afterwards."

She flinched at the harshness of his words, at the anger and the raw desire which had provoked them.

"Oh, don't worry," he gibed. "I won't defile you again— and you can always go and take another bath. But why the sudden transformation? I think I'm entitled to ask that."

Her voice shook. "I don't think you're entitled to ask anything, but if you must know it was your calm assumption that I was prepared to be yet another of your conquests. You asked me not to make you wait any longer, the implication being that I'd already kept you waiting longer than you were used to."

"Is that a fact?" he said slowly. He took a packet of cigarettes from his pocket and lit one, resuming his seat on the edge of the dressing table, almost visibly allowing the tension and the anger to drain out of him. At last he said, "If that's the impression I gave you, Ginny, it wasn't intentional. Believe it or not, I don't regard you or any other woman as just another notch in the bedpost. Let's forget the whole thing and begin again at the beginning, shall we?" He paused. "Ginny, please have dinner with me tonight?"

He saw her give a slight start, and his voice gentled. "Just dinner—no strings, I promise. We'll talk about the weather, about books—the state of the union, anything you want. And I won't kiss you or lay a finger on you unless you give me leave."

Ginny barely heard what he was saying. Her mind was filled with the image of the dinner party she had given, which she had cooked for, and how she had found Vivien Lanyon in his arms when it was over. Vivien Lanyon, the woman he was going to marry.

"Ginny." His voice was half laughing, half a groan. "What must I do to convince you? Ask your great-aunt along as chaperone?"

"And what must I do to convince you?" she said stonily. "I don't want to have dinner with you. And you shouldn't want it either."

"May I ask why not?" He drew deeply on his cigarette.

She was at a loss to know how to answer him. If she mentioned Mrs. Lanyon's name, then he would know that she had been gossiping with someone, and he would not be pleased to know that his most personal affairs were the talk of the locality.

She took a deep breath. "Because if you know that you belong to someone, in your heart, then that's the only person you should want to be with," she said lamely.

"And in your heart I suppose you feel you belong to my cousin Toby," he said with a kind of controlled savagery.

An indignant denial was trembling on her lips, when she realised that if it was ever uttered, then he would demand another explanation for her halting words. And she wasn't sure whether she could even hint at the subject of his future marriage without self-betrayal, which was unthinkable, she told herself. Better, far better, for him to believe that his own explanation was the truth, and that she was nursing a hopeless passion for Toby. After all, she thought, her nails digging into the palms of her hands, it could so easily have been the truth. She had even managed to convince herself at one stage that it was Toby she wanted.

She said in a low voice, "I can't help myself. I'm sorry."

Max said bitterly, "You're sorry." He walked past her and out of the room, slamming the door behind him.

Ginny sank down on to the dressing stool, her legs suddenly refusing to support her. Over and over she told herself that she had done the right thing, but the words sounded hollow and unconvincing, even to herself.

WHEN she eventually went downstairs she found Aunt Mary alone. Tim, it seemed, had been whisked off somewhere in the car with Max.

"I have no idea where they've gone. Max simply said they would be back later," said Aunt Mary, casting a shrewd glance at Ginny's pallor and downcast eyes. "I thought dear Max seemed a little put out," she added meditatively. Then with apparent irrelevance, "Did you you enjoy your soup, dear?"

"What? I'm sorry." Ginny came out of a rather troublous reverie with a start. "I'm afraid I didn't have much of the soup. I wasn't really hungry," she apologised. "I—I think I'll get Muffin's basket, and his rubber bone and things, and put them out of sight. I don't want Tim to be upset again when he returns."

"Oh, Max has already seen to all that, dear, while Tim was upstairs washing his face," Aunt Mary said briskly. "And he came to some arrangement with Mr. Henderson over the value of the animals that were killed. You will naturally want to repay him."

"Naturally," Ginny echoed wearily. "Barbie hasn't come back with the car yet?"

"No, she has not." Aunt Mary's lips were set in lines of disapproval. "I can't think where she's got to. I'd have imagined she would have seen all there was to see in Market Harford in half an hour. She has no thought, no consideration for anyone but herself."

Ginny sighed. "Perhaps, but it must be very quiet for her here compared with the kind of life she enjoys in London. And she couldn't know what was going to happen—this afternoon. None of us foresaw that," she added with difficulty.

Barbie did not return until supper was long over. Tim had reappeared in the meantime, looking slightly dazed, with the news that Max had taken him to the Manor and thrown him up on the back of one of the tallest mares in the stables for his first riding lesson. Although this had consisted of being led round and round the paddock at a walk, he could still proudly boast that he hadn't fallen off once.

"And the ground was ever such a long way away," he added triumphantly. His recital of his prowess was eventually interrupted by Barbie's arrival. She came in smiling, and tossed the car keys on to the table in front of Ginny.

"It's time you traded in that old heap and got something decent to drive, darling," she said carelessly. "By the way, it needs petrol. I almost drained the tank getting home." She sat down at the table. "If those are sausages, then no, thanks. I had something to eat in the town. If there's some hot water, I might have a bath. It's been raining, and I got caught in it on my way back to the car park."

"Ginevra," Aunt Mary said pointedly, "also got wet this afternoon. Very wet. She had to go out in search of the dog."

"Oh, did she?" Barbie's tone was bored. "Well, rather her than me, I can tell you. He raced past me as I was getting in the car. I called to him, but he took not a blind bit of notice, disobedient little brute. Did you find him in the end?"

"In the end," Ginny said bleakly. Out of the corner of her eye she saw Tim, very white, lay down his knife and fork and get up from the table. She waited until the door had closed behind him, then said, "Muffin's dead, Barbie. He was shot by one of the local farmers for sheep worrying."

For a moment her sister looked genuinely taken aback. "Good God, I'd no idea. What a shame! Poor old Muff. He was more Tim's dog than yours, though, wasn't he?"

"Yes," Ginny acknowledged. "I'm afraid Tim's going to take it hard. I hope he doesn't start having nightmares again."

"Amen to that," Barbie said briskly. She rose, "I'll go and see about that bath."

Tim did not come downstairs again that evening, and when Ginny peeped into his room on her way to bed, telltale stains on his cheeks revealed that he had cried himself to sleep.

She went on to her own room and walked across to the window to draw the curtains. Max's car was missing from the courtyard, as it had been all evening. She guessed he must have dropped Tim at the door and gone straight out again, probably back to the Manor, she thought. Although he had appeared not to understand what she had meant earlier, perhaps he had belatedly applied her words to Vivien Lanyon and himself. And after all, she had deliberately tried to drive him away. She really could not complain, she thought desolately, if he had taken her at her word and gone....

She was thankful that she had the weekend to face, and not a day shut up in the study with Max. She made herself keep busy, so that she wouldn't have time to sit and think and be unhappy. She did some work in the garden, and took Tim into Market Harford with her to do the weekend shopping, then on to a re-showing of an old James Bond film which he had never seen. He was still subdued, but he appeared to enjoy the film, and when they came out of the cinema they came face-to-face with Toby.

Just for a moment Ginny thought he looked rather taken aback to see them, then he was laughing and ruffling Tim's hair, and offering to buy them tea at the White Hart, and she thought she must have been mistaken.

It was a pleasant old-fashioned sort of tea with lots of buttery toast and home-made cakes, and Tim's appetite rocketed back to normal, Ginny noticed with a thankful heart. She had managed to warn Toby about Muffin's sad fate, and he had been suitably sympathetic, and kept the conversation carefully steered away from the animal kingdom. In the end it was Tim who talked about animals, reverting to the subject of his first riding lesson with great glee. When at last he wandered off with a handful of coins in search of a fruit machine, Toby turned to Ginny with a faint smile.

"Cousin Max in a noble mood. How very uncharacteristic," he said lightly.

She said an abstracted, "Yes," then, "Toby, is this new job of yours going to be based in London?"

"No, Birmingham, actually. Why do you ask?"

"I was wondering what you'd do about your flat. Wondering actually if I could—sub-let it for a while."

Toby gave a slight whistle. "My God, don't say you've decided to kick over the family traces at last! There's hope for you yet, sweetie."

"Oh, no." She stared at him. "I didn't mean that. I—I'm looking for another job, you see, and it would make life much easier if I knew Tim and Aunt Mary had a roof over their heads while I was looking. I'd pay whatever rent you wanted, of course, and...."

"No, Ginny." He shook his head, his smile charming and rueful. "No way, darling. Tim's a great kid, of course, and I adore your aunt, but I thought I'd made my opinion of ready-made families quite clear."

"But what has that to do with it?" she asked desperately. "I'm not suggesting that we move in with you. I'd probably only need the place for a couple of weeks—while I find another job, and somewhere to live.''

''On a secretary's wage?'' He lifted his brows sceptically. ''Pie in the sky, Ginny. Castles in Spain. Anyway, what's wrong with the job you've got? I know Max can be a swine, but he's a rich swine, and he won't be around for ever. He'll be back in California or off to the Bahamas or somewhere before you know it, and you'll have Monk's Dower to yourself again. You can vegetate in peace.''

''Max's next trip anywhere will probably be his honeymoon.'' She tried to speak naturally. ''And his wife to be has already made it clear that she intends to dispense with my services. I'd rather resign than be fired by Mrs. Lanyon.''

''Meaning Mrs. Lanyon intends to become Mrs. Hendrick.'' Toby gave her a sharp look. ''Well, good luck to her. She isn't the first to imagine she's hooked him by any means, and it's my bet she won't be the last either. My dear cousin likes his independence too much.''

Ginny said in a small voice, ''Was that what Laura Hertford thought? That he would marry her?''

''Laura?'' Toby raised his brows. ''God knows what she thought, if she ever did think. She was always getting steamed up over some man or another, neurotic little bitch.''

Ginny stared at him. ''But I thought—I mean, you said she took an overdose, because of Max. Isn't it true?''

He shrugged, looking uncomfortable. ''Why, yes. At least, that's what was assumed—what everyone was saying.''

''I see.'' Ginny felt a little sick. ''I hadn't realised you were just passing on gossip—scandal. Thanks for the tea, Toby. We'd better be going.''

He stood up with her. ''Think over what I've said, Ginny. If you want to sow a few of those wild oats you mentioned, and think the flat would be a suitable base, then you're more than welcome, but I draw the line at dependent relatives. You do understand, don't you, sweetie?''

"Yes," she said, "I understand perfectly." It took an effort to return his smile, but she managed it somehow.

Driving back through the lanes to Monk's Dower, Tim was in a talkative mood, and although Ginny would have preferred to have been quiet with her own disturbing thoughts, she was so glad to see him restored to something like his usual spirits that she joined in gladly with his eager discussion of the various ways in which the villains of the film they had just seen had met their doom.

"The tea was great too," Tim remarked after a pause. "The cakes were nearly as good as yours, Mouse."

"Thank you," Ginny drily acknowledged this generous praise.

"You like Toby, don't you?" She was aware of Tim's unwinking stare fixed on her as he put the question.

"Yes, of course," she said after the briefest of hesitations. It was true, she thought. She did like him. It was not, after all, his fault if he failed to live up to the idealised image that her lonely heart had created.

"Do you like him better than Max?" the Grand Inquisitor at her side persisted.

"It's hard to say," she said feebly, after a much longer pause. "I—I work for Max, you see, whereas Toby's just—a friend."

"I used to like Toby best," Tim said slowly. "But that was before Max came really. I like Monk's Dower, now. And I like Max. He doesn't go out of his way to make a fuss of you like Toby does, but underneath he really cares what happens to you."

Ginny's heart sank. She said gently, "Tim love, what happens to us isn't really Max's concern, you know. And Monk's Dower doesn't belong to him or to us. We—we may have to leave soon and look for somewhere else to live."

"I don't want to live anywhere else," Tim protested. "And Max is concerned about us, whatever you say."

Glancing at him, Ginny saw that his face had flushed as red as a beetroot. He said in a hurry, "I wasn't going to tell you this because Max said I wasn't to. He said you'd only get upset and worried, and that you had enough on your plate as it was, but I must tell you because it proves what I've said." He sent her a shamefaced look. "I—I started nicking off from school."

"Nicking off?" Ginny echoed, bewildered. "You mean—playing truant? But when—and where did you go?"

Tim shrugged. "Just round about. I used to go out for the school bus in the mornings just as usual, and miss it on purpose. Only Max saw me one day and the next time I did it, he was waiting, and he said if I ever did it again, or anything as stupid for that matter, he'd give me such a hiding that I wouldn't be able to sit down for a week. That was when he said about not wanting you to be more worried than you were already. So you see, he does care about us, Ginny. And he made me take my homework round to him so that he could check up on me, and see that I was working," he ended with a little rush.

"Dear God," Ginny muttered, half under her breath. She found herself completely shaken by Tim's confession, and its implications.

"Are you angry with me, Mouse?" Tim asked anxiously.

"No," she said ruefully. "Angry with myself. Angry that a stranger should have known more about what was going on in my family than I did myself."

"Max isn't a stranger," Tim protested. "He's our friend."

Trying to keep her voice steady, she said, "He's my boss, Tim. Don't please build any more on it than that."

They arrived back at Monk's Dower to find Barbie sullen and Aunt Mary icily furious in an atmosphere that could be cut with a knife. Ginny learned that the trouble had started because Barbie had spent most of the afternoon on the telephone.

"Interfering old cat," her sister stormed, when they were alone together in the bedroom. "She actually had the nerve to ask me when I was going to get another job. My God, if it were only that easy! There are far more shows closing than there are opening. Doesn't she realise that?"

"I don't think she knows very much about the theatre, any more than I do," Ginny said temperately.

"Well, there's some excuse for her—but none at all for you." Barbie swung round to vent some of her ill temper on her sister. "God, you only work for the decade's leading playwright, that's all. Will you be seeing Max this weekend? Don't you have to go over to his side of the house to make the beds or something?"

"No, I don't have any work to do there until Monday." Ginny tried to smile. "Don't you think I put in enough hours as it is?"

"Heaven knows how long you spend on your dreary little chores," Barbie said sourly. "But when you do see him next, you could make some discreet enquiries about this play that you're typing for him. In other words, Mouse, find out if there's going to be a part for me or not."

"Barbie!" Ginny was appalled. "I couldn't!"

"You mean you won't," her sister snapped back. "Right then, I'll ask him myself. He owes me a favour, after all."

"I don't really see how you make that out," Ginny said wearily.

Barbie sent her an acidly sweet smile. "Why, for permitting my baby sister to become his tame factotum, of course," she drawled. "What else?"

Ginny gave her a defeated look before she turned away and went downstairs to attempt to soothe Aunt Mary's ruffled feathers.

In an effort to divert her attention from Barbie's misdemeanours, she told her briefly about Tim's confession, and was amazed to see her great-aunt nod rather grimly.

"So that was it!" she exclaimed. "I had a feeling that Tim was up to something. A teacher's instinct, I suppose. He needs a firmer hand than we can provide, my dear."

"Oh, Aunt Mary!" Ginny stared at her, distressed. "What do you suggest? That we should tell the local Social Services department and perhaps find foster-parents for Tim? He'd hate it, and so would I."

Aunt Mary sighed, leaning back wearily in her chair.

"That might be an ultimate solution. We can't ignore the fact that Tim is coming up to a difficult age, and we must be thankful that Max was able to nip the first signs of trouble in the bud."

Ginny said, "Yes," in a subdued tone, failing to notice the keen glance her great-aunt sent her.

When supper was over and cleared away, Ginny decided that she had to take the bull by the horns. Things, she told herself firmly, could not go on as they were any longer. She would have to see Max and tell him so. No doubt his intervention in their affairs had been kindly meant, but it was now proving yet another burden for her. Monk's Dower, she thought unhappily, would have been far easier to leave if he had held them all at arm's length, and refused to become involved with them on any level whatsoever.

And what about you? a sly voice mocked inside her head. Are you really trying to tell yourself that you too wanted to be kept at arm's length? Aren't you glad that it was Max Hendrick who was the first to teach you how it feels to be a woman?

No, her heart cried out in anguish. Not if I'd known that his lovemaking would leave me lonelier than ever—if I'd known how much he could make me want him, or how miserable I would be.

And there was nothing to look forward to except more misery, more loneliness and an ache deep inside her, a yearning that only Max could satisfy, except that she could never let it happen. She had to leave Monk's Dower, and leave soon, while she still had her self-respect to bolster her.

She found notepaper and an envelope and wrote out her resignation with a steady hand, giving as her reason for leaving the need to find a job with more permanency about it.

She was just about to open the communicating door when it swung open from the other side and Barbie appeared.

"He's not there," she said coolly. "But he'll be back, and

not alone either. There's a bottle of vintage champagne waiting on ice in the drawing room and two glasses. If he hasn't invited you round to drink to the completion of the new play, sister dear, I'd say he had something else to celebrate, wouldn't you?''

Ginny forced a smile. "I did warn you."

"Yes, you did, clever little Ginny." Barbie's eyes surveyed her almost insolently, taking in the faint flush on her sister's cheekbones. "And something tells me that you aren't quite as indifferent to the sexy Mr. Hendrick as you like everyone to believe. Poor Ginny, what a man to choose to cut your milk teeth on! Well, I'm not going to spend my evening moping over the might-have-beens. I'm going into Market Harford. I suppose you won't be using the car."

"No, you can take it." Ginny sighed inwardly at the thought of the full petrol tank she had provided that afternoon. "But I don't know what you'll find to do there."

Barbie's eyes were full of mockery. "Oh, there'll be something, Mouse. Even Market Harford must make some concessions to the twentieth century on Saturday night. I believe there's even a disco of sorts. It could be amusing."

"Amusing to watch the yokels enjoying themselves," Ginny said drily.

She went straight to the study and left the envelope containing her resignation on Max's desk. She took a long look round before she left the room. At least the play was almost finished, she thought. And one day, probably miles from here, she would pick up a newspaper and read about its first night, and that Max Hendrick had another hit on his hands. She had no doubt it would be a success. There would be champagne then, too, she thought, and Vivien Lanyon would be with him, only they would probably be married by then. It would be her right to share in his success.

But it isn't his success that I care about, she thought. It's his happiness. And perhaps one day I shall think about him being happy with Vivien Lanyon, and be able to bear it. But not yet. Not now.

She didn't even glance into the drawing room as she went

back into her own part of the house. She didn't need to check on Barbie's story. She knew the champagne would be waiting there, just as she had said, and why it was there, and that was pain enough.

Be happy, my love, she whispered as she went past the door. Oh, be happy.

CHAPTER NINE

SHE was in a corridor full of locked doors, and no matter how loudly she knocked, or how often she implored some-one to open one of them for her, they remained locked against her. Somewhere behind one of them was the haven that she sought, the only haven in the world for her, but how could she find it behind so many closed doors?

She saw the door at the far end of the corridor slowly begin to open, and she ran to it, but however fast she ran, it still remained at the same distance. There was a man stand-ing in the doorway with his back turned to her and she knew it was Max, and she called his name, but he did not turn and look at her, and she cried out once again in utter despair. And then it seemed as if the doorway was only a few yards away, but as she reached it Vivien Lanyon stepped out of nowhere and slammed the door, laughing, in her face.

Ginny said imploringly, "No, Max! No!" And it was her own voice she heard, and she was sitting bolt upright in her own bed in her own room in the darkness.

Immediately she glanced at the adjoining bed. It was im-possible for her not to have woken Barbie, but as her eyes accustomed themselves to the gloom, she saw that the bed was empty. For a moment she thought that Barbie might have gone to the bathroom, and that it might have been her movements which had disturbed her, but it was clear that her sister's bed had not been occupied at all. It was still as neat as when she herself had made it earlier that day.

She pushed back her covers, and swung her feet to the floor, struck by a pang of anxiety. Barbie in the car, in the darkness, coming back from Market Harford through twisting lanes she did not know very well. She went over to the window and looked out, and gave a swift sigh of relief. The car was there. So where was Barbie? Surely no local disco went on until the early hours of the morning. Perhaps she was in the kitchen making herself a bedtime drink.

Ginny picked up her dressing gown and put it on. That was an excellent idea, she thought. A milky drink was just what she needed to help her back to peaceful sleep again. Noiselessly, not wanting to disturb Aunt Mary in the next room who was normally a light sleeper, she went out on to the landing and down the stairs. She went slowly, feeling her way, because she didn't want to put on the lights, then paused. There was light coming from the sitting room, through the door which stood slightly ajar. Light—and the murmur of voices. Barbie was not alone.

For a moment Ginny stood on the bottom step, frozen with indignation. However she might live her life in London, Barbie had no right to bring some stranger back to Monk's Dower in the middle of the night. She took an impetuous step forward, then stopped again, her attention riveted by the long trail of colour spilling over the threshold of the room. She recognised it at once. It was the violet dress which Barbie had been wearing as she left the house.

Ginny's hands crept up to her mouth, and a wave of embarrassed heat swept over her body. There could only be one reason why her sister's dress should be lying on the floor. The soft murmurs and other noises which were reaching her ears were assuming a very definite meaning too, and it needed no imagination at all to know what was taking place behind that half-closed sitting-room door.

She turned away, feeling slightly sick, intending to go back upstairs and pray that no one else in the household had woken. She could imagine Aunt Mary's reaction if she had come down and stumbled on this sordid little scene.

But the dress was not all Barbie had discarded. As Ginny turned, she stumbled against something lying on the floor—a high-heeled shoe, which shot away across the polished floor with a clatter that to Ginny's over-sensitive ears sounded like machine gun fire.

She stood at the foot of the stairs, transfixed, and heard quite plainly Toby say sharply, "What the hell was that?" And then, "No, don't move, darling. I'll go and see for myself."

Toby and her sister—there together, making love, and at any moment Toby was going to walk into the hall and see her standing there like some awful Peeping Tom.

If she fled up the stairs, they would hear her. She looked round wildly for some other refuge, and saw the communicating door only a yard or so away. In two silent steps she had reached it, and was through it, and standing in the darkness on the other side.

She could hear the two of them talking quite plainly, neither of them apparently in the least concerned with keeping their voices down. Toby was swearing that he'd heard something, and Barbie was teasing him about his nerves. She knew instinctively from the way they were speaking that this was far from being simply a casual encounter, and that they had been on intimate terms for some time.

In a way it was a relief. She had been so afraid that Barbie was there with someone she had met only that night. But in other ways it was a hideous embarrassment, because apart from everything else it meant that here she was on Max's side of the house, trapped. She wished she had either the sophistication or the nerve to walk back through the communicating door, through the hall and up the stairs to her room, wishing them a civil good morning in passing, but she had neither, and she knew she would rather die than let them know she had discovered the truth about their relationship.

She counted to a hundred slowly, but she could still hear them talking and laughing softly when she opened the door a crack, and she realised there was no way she could pass the sitting room unnoticed.

Her feet were becoming colder by the second, and she

wished she had stopped to put her slippers on before ven-
turing downstairs. She shivered. It could be some time before they became sufficiently absorbed in each other once
again not to notice her quiet retreat back to her room, she
thought, so she might as well make herself reasonably comfortable while she was waiting. She certainly had little wish
to stand here in the dark listening to them making love.

She went down the passage, and paused at the drawing-
room door before pushing it open gently and going in. She
tried not to look at the empty bottle and the two used glasses
on the low table. The celebration had duly taken place, it
seemed, and she had to face the fact that Vivien Lanyon
might at this very moment be asleep in Max's arms upstairs.

There were still some embers glowing a dull red in the
hearth and she added a few judicious pieces of wood, coax-
ing them into a small blaze. She sat on the rug for a while,
watching the play of the blue and gold flames, and hearing
the comforting crackle of the dry wood as it caught. She
wondered how long she would have to wait, and wished she
had brought her watch as well.

She'd wait for half an hour, she thought, and then go
back. She took one of the cushions from the sofa and lay
down on the rug, wrapping her dressing gown round her
bare feet. She lay still, watching the flames, and trying to
count the passage of time in her head, but it wasn't easy
because she kept losing count and having to start again.
Every part of her body was beginning to feel curiously
weightless, she noticed detachedly, with the exception of
her eyelids, which felt like lead. She had no intention of
going to sleep, of course, but no one could surely blame her
for dozing a little because this half hour was beginning to
seem endless. She allowed her eyes to close. Just for a moment, she told herself drowsily. Only for a moment.

She began counting seconds in her head again, but long
before she reached sixty, someone was shaking her, bringing her back from the warm golden world which had closed
so thankfully round her.

She said with dignity, "I'm not really asleep," and she

opened her eyes to a dazzle of light. She blinked up into Max's face.

"Like hell you're not," he said drily. He was kneeling beside her, wearing as far as she could judge nothing except that brief towelling bathrobe of his. He was unshaven and tousled and he looked distinctly annoyed.

He said, "Perhaps you'd like to explain what you're doing here at four in the morning, Ginevra. I don't flatter myself that you've changed your mind about sleeping with me. Are you ill?"

"No," she denied hastily. She sat up, swallowing. "Is it really four o'clock? I—I'd better go back."

"Certainly," he said pleasantly. "After you give me the explanation to which I think I'm entitled. Do you walk in your sleep, or is this another bid to catch pneumonia, following your escapade in the rain?"

Ginny said wretchedly, "I didn't mean for you to find me. I was only going to stay for a little while. I—I couldn't sleep, that's all."

"You were out for the count," he commented. "I probably wouldn't have found you until breakfast-time if that damned car hadn't woken me and I'd not come down to investigate."

"Car?" she echoed, fixing her eyes on his face with painful intensity. "You heard a car leave?"

"Yes," he said, frowning. "I know your establishment doesn't go in for late visitors, and it occurred to me there might have been a prowler."

She gave a little groan. She'd been asleep for nearly two hours, it seemed, and now Toby had departed and Barbie would have gone up to the bedroom and discovered her empty bed.

She exclaimed, "Oh, this is terrible!" and began to scramble to her feet, disentangling herself with difficulty from the folds of her dressing gown. Max took her arm as she turned towards the door.

"You're not making much sense, Ginny. What's so terrible?"

She looked at him, almost distractedly. "I found them together, you see. They didn't see me, but I fell over one of Barbie's shoes, and it made a noise, and I couldn't get back upstairs in time, so I came in here."

"Whom did you find, and where?" he said patiently.

"I've told you." Ginny almost wrung her hands. "You see, her bed was empty. That's what made me go downstairs in the first place. I thought she might be ill, or something. Then I heard them talking, and I realised—what was going on. I know it's prudish and silly, but I felt if they saw me, I'd never be able to face either of them again."

"Your sister was downstairs with someone? With a man, presumably, who has just left. Is that what you're trying to say?"

She said, "Yes," her voice practically inaudible. And, "She was with Toby."

Max said very wearily, "Oh, God." There was a long silence, then suddenly he moved, putting his arm round her, drawing her close. Ginny went to him unresistingly, closing her eyes and resting her cheek against the hair-roughened skin of his chest. Eventually she heard him swear softly under his breath.

She said softly, "They're lovers, aren't they, Max, and you knew it."

"Yes, I knew, but I didn't intend you should find out. It's not serious, of course. I shouldn't think it ever is with either of them. Toby's a worthless little swine, but he can charm birds from trees when he wants, and I knew you'd fallen pretty heavily," he said harshly. "To give him his due he didn't know you were sisters when he first came down here. One of the reasons he came was because they'd had a flaming row and she'd kicked him out. They were living together at the time." He paused. "He'd have probably thought it quite amusing to have seduced you down here, while he was still having an affair with your sister in London."

Ginny shivered, and his hand came up and began to stroke her hair.

He said, "I don't think he bargained for her actually turning up here. And I'd already given him due warning that I was on to his little game and that if he treated you badly, it would give me the greatest pleasure to break his lecherous little neck. When I collected your sister at the station that day, I told her what the situation was, and hinted that it might be worth her while to make you believe that she and Toby were just casual acquaintances. I don't think she knew if I was offering to become a substitute lover, or arranging an audition for her, and I'm sure she didn't care much."

Ginny said in a muffled voice, "She probably didn't."

Max said savagely, "I could kill them both! Surely they could have waited until they got back to town before leaping on each other again. I wanted Toby to fade quietly out of your life. That way you'd have been hurt least, or that's what I hoped anyway. And now it's all gone wrong. Poor little Ginny!"

The tenderness in his voice was her undoing, and she began to cry quietly because even though he was only holding her to comfort her because he believed she was breaking her heart over Toby, nevertheless there was an exquisite happiness in being in his arm's which was altogether too much to bear.

After a while he said, "You'd better go home, Ginny, before you're missed."

"I'll have been missed already. Barbie will have seen my empty bed," she said in a low voice. "Max, I can't face her. Let me stay here for the rest of the night. I can sleep on the sofa."

There was a pause, then he sighed. "No, you can spend what's left of the night upstairs in my room. I'll use the sofa."

He picked her up as if she had been a child and carried her out of the room and up the stairs. He laid her in the middle of the big bed and drew the duvet over her, and she leaned back against the pillows, staring up at him and wondering how he could look at her and not guess the truth.

He said, "Can I get you anything? I don't have any sleeping pills, but a warm drink might help."

"Yes," she said, "it might." Max went away to get it, and she lay back against his pillow and tried to think, but the time for thinking seemed past. Her emotions were directing her now, telling her to take what she wanted and accept whatever regrets might follow.

When he returned, he brought a beaker of hot chocolate, and, as she had hoped, he sat on the edge of the bed while she drank it. She watched him from beneath her lashes, as she sipped the chocolate. His face was brooding and a little bitter, as if none of his own thoughts appealed to him. She wanted to say something, but there didn't seem to be any words. When the chocolate was finished, he took the beaker from her and stood up.

She said very quickly before her courage failed her. "Max—please don't go. Stay with me. I don't want to be alone."

He said explosively, "My God!" Then, "You don't want much, do you Ginevra?"

"I'm sorry," she faltered. "I thought...."

"I don't think I want to know what you thought. It wouldn't be very flattering to either of us," he interrupted. He stood for a long moment looking down at her, as if he was conducting some fierce inward struggle, then he said with a brief sigh, "All right, Ginny, if it's what you want." He put out a hand to the bedside lamp and plunged the room into darkness.

She lay very still, holding her breath, aware of the sudden pounding of her heart and the dryness of her mouth. She realised she was still wearing her dressing gown over her nightdress and wondered if she should have taken one or both of them off. Or would he do that for her? He knew, of course, that this was the first time for her, and he would make allowances. At least she hoped he would, she thought desperately, as the mattress beside her shifted beneath his weight.

Max said almost wearily, "Relax, Ginny. There's nothing

to be afraid of. You didn't want to sleep alone—well, you shan't. But you are going to sleep, and so, please God, am I.''

She lay rigidly beside him and let the darkness close round her, staring into it with eyes that saw only shadows. Her hands were clenched into fists of frustration. She ached with wanting him, and with the bewilderment of being denied her heart's desire. He had wanted her; he had asked her to come to him. Now he was rejecting her, and a muffled sob rose in her throat.

She heard him groan softly, then he reached for her, pulling her against him, moulding her slenderness to the warm curve of his body. Ginny turned her face against him, feeling the warm strong beat of his heart under her cheek.

She bit on her bottom lip fiercely, resisting the impulse to put her mouth against his skin, to caress and fondle him as he had caressed her only a few hours earlier. The fear of a further rejection was too strong in her.

If there was no passion, she thought, at least she was in his arms, and didn't they say that half a loaf was better than no bread at all, particularly when you were faced with a lifetime of famine. And eventually she slept, as Max had said she would.

She had slept deeply, too, she realised when she opened her eyes to find the room filled with sunlight, and the bed beside her empty. She had not been aware of him leaving her. She sat up, pushing the the hair out of her eyes, and saw the piece of paper on the adjoining pillow. The message was brief and to the point. He had gone to fetch the papers, and when he returned they would talk. She could put the coffee on. He was hers, Max.

She gave a little shaken laugh. On paper, he never wasted a word. There was only one slight ambiguity—that word which spoke of belonging. He was not hers, and never would be, and that presumably was what he wanted to talk about on his return.

She got up, and made the bed slowly, remembering that first evening in this very room, her hostility, the resentment which had not merely been sparked by the fact that he

was not Toby, she realised now, but because even then she
had been aware of his attraction, and had fought against it.

It was a fight I should have won, she thought, sighing.

She heard the front door open and shut downstairs, and
hurried out on to the landing.

"I haven't made the coffee," she called out as she went
down the stairs. "I only woke up a few minutes ago
and...."

Her voice trailed away into appalled silence as her eyes
met the hostile, icy gaze of Vivien Lanyon, standing in the
hall below.

There was a long terrible silence, then Mrs. Lanyon said
viciously, "Slut!"

"No, please!" Ginny gripped the bannister rail until her
knuckles turned white. "It isn't what you think, Mrs. Lanyon, I promise you. Something—upset me last night, and
Max let me sleep here, that's all."

"Liar!" Vivien Lanyon spat at her. "Do you think I
haven't noticed the way you've looked at him, in spite of
that milk and water façade of yours? My God, I must have
been mad ever to hire you! I'd forgotten the effect all that
youth and phony innocence can have on the most experienced man. Well, you're sacked, do you hear me? You can
pack your things and get out of Monk's Dower!"

"I'm already leaving," Ginny said. She was shaking so
violently, she thought she might collapse. "My resignation
is on Max's desk. It's been there for twenty-four hours."

"Which is exactly the time you've got to get out of
here," Vivien Lanyon snapped. Her face looked naked and
ugly under the carefully applied cosmetics. The things she
was saying were naked and ugly, too, and Ginny put her
hands over her ears to shut them out, and then Max was
there, coming swiftly and silently down the passage from
the communicating door, and her shame was complete.

She closed her eyes, turning away, trying to blot the
whole scene out of her mind. She heard the front door slam
and winced. Max came upstairs and his hands bruised her
arms as he turned her inexorably to face him.

"She's gone, Ginny," he said quietly. "It's all right now."

"I'm sorry," she said with a little moan. "I thought it was you. I didn't want to make trouble for you. I'd have stayed upstairs."

"You haven't made trouble," he said. "I've no doubt Vivien's cupidity will win in the end. And her solicitor's a good man. He'll make her see sense."

"You make it sound so cold-blooded," she whispered.

He raised his eyebrows. "I've never considered buying a house to be a particularly emotional experience," he said, looking faintly amused.

"Buying a house?" Ginny was totally bewildered. "Another one?"

"This house." He put a hand and smoothed her dishevelled hair back from her forehead. "I've finally got Vivien to agree to sell me Monk's Dower. We shook hands on it last night."

"Sell it to you?" she echoed stupidly. "But it would have been yours anyway when you were married."

"Thanks," he said drily. "But I'm not prepared to go to those lengths, even for Monk's Dower."

She still did not understand. It was beyond her, and with a little defeated shake of her head she made to move past him and go downstairs. He detained her, his hand on her arm.

"Now where are you going?"

"To pack," she said drearily. "Surely you heard her firing me? I thought perhaps if I left today, she might let Aunt Mary and Tim stay on for a few days until I can find somewhere for them."

"There is somewhere for them," said Max on a note of anger. "They can move in here, and you with them."

"I can't, " she said raggedly. "She'll be so angry. She won't let you have the house. It will spoil everything between you."

"It will spoil nothing, because there is nothing," he said. "And if she's fool enough to turn down my offer for the house, then there'll be another one. It was just that I thought you loved the place, that you looked on it as your home."

"I have no home," she said in a low voice.

"You could have if you married me," he said. "I found your letter of resignation in the study, and I can appreciate your desire for a more permanent post. Marriage is the most permanent thing I can think of."

Colour swamped her face. "You're laughing at me!"

"I've never been further from laughter in my life," he said flatly. "You want to be safe, secure—well, that's what I'm offering you. And the deal includes your great-aunt and Tim as well, but that goes without saying."

Ginny's eyes went wonderingly to his face, taking in every harsh line. His eyes were hooded, enigmatic as they watched her.

She said breathlessly, "No—no, I couldn't." She tried to push past him, stumbling a little on the hem of her dressing gown, and he cursed swiftly and picked her up in his arms, walking down the stairs holding her, and shouldering his way into the drawing room.

He sat down on the sofa, still holding her in his arms. His voice was grave as he said, "Last night you came to me for comfort, Ginny. What's changed?"

Nothing had changed, she thought in agony. It had not been Max's comfort she had wanted, it had been his love. And without it, she would have to pay too high a price for the safety and security he was offering.

She tried to smile, "Marriage is a little more than just comfort."

"I thought that might be it," he said wryly. "As I attempted to demonstrate last night, I won't make any demands on you which you can't fulfil, Ginny. I'm prepared to wait until you get bloody Toby out of your bloodstream. I understand he's gone back to London, by the way, and your sister with him, it seems. Your aunt says all her things have gone from your room, so you won't have either of them to face."

"But I have Aunt Mary to face," she muttered, struggling vainly to be free. "She'll be furious with me."

"She was a little put out, naturally, but when I explained that we were going to be married, she soon came round. Tim thinks it's a great idea too. The only one I have to convince is you. Marry me, Ginny. You wanted a roof over your head, I'm offering you one."

"That isn't what I want," she flared at him.

"No?" Max threw his head back and looked at her unsmilingly "So tell me about it. Is it Toby?"

"No!" she nearly yelled. "It isn't. It never has been."

"Then why the hell did you let me think it was?" demanded Max with equal violence. "Look at me, Ginny, and stop pretending."

"There was Vivien Lanyon," she mumbled.

"No, there wasn't. There was you, Ginevra, and there always has been, from that very first night when you threw my dinner at me. You walked into that kitchen with your eyes shining like a million stars, and a smile which said the world belonged to you. I'd forgotten women could look like that and mean it. An unrestricted diet of actresses tends to dull the palate," he added with a twist of his mouth. "I could have wrung your neck when I found that look was meant for Toby. I knew him too well. I swore that one day I'd make you look at me like that, but I never did. You never have."

"Until now," she whispered, staring up into his dark face with all her heart in her eyes.

He drew one swift sharp breath, then his mouth was on hers, possessing and demanding with a fierce urgency which made her blood sing in her veins. She clung to him in utter abandonment, returning kiss for kiss with total ardour.

She was breathless when he released her mouth, and she reached up smiling to wind her arms round his neck and draw him down to her again. His lips lingered and burned, and she was on fire for him, her body arching in silent supplication for his caresses.

"I hope you're not planning a long engagement," he murmured against her lips, and she gave a shaken little laugh.

After a while she said in a small voice, "But, Max, you did kiss Mrs. Lanyon after the dinner party. I saw you. And her car was there all night."

"But she wasn't," he told her. "Her car wouldn't start, so I drove her home in mine, and got the garage to come the following morning. And yes, I kissed her because she made it very plain she expected it, and I was feeling pretty raw over you that particular evening. I thought I could use her as a palliative, but it didn't work. It was you I wanted in my arms!"

"Then why—" Ginny paused, suddenly shy. "Why didn't you make love to me last night?"

"Because I was still afraid that it was Toby you loved," he said huskily. "You'd given such a good imitation of it for so long. And that's why I offered you marriage on the terms I did—because I thought it was the only way it would be acceptable to you. I don't suppose I'd have been the first man to start courting his wife after the ceremony." He paused, then said, "About Laura...."

"You don't have to tell me," she said.

"But I want to." He placed a finger on her lips. "She was quite young and very unhappy, and she came to work for me on the recommendation of a friend who was acting as her psychiatrist. He warned me that there would be problems. Her parents had just got divorced after many years of apparently happy marriage, and the man she'd been living with had become hopelessly addicted to heroin. That overdose she took wasn't the first attempt she'd made to kill herself, nor was it prompted by anything I'd done. It's important to me that you believe that."

"I do believe you," Ginny told him. "Toby admitted to me that the story he'd told me had been pure speculation. I felt dreadful. I'd misjudged you so often and so deliberately." She bent her head. "It was easier to let myself think you were just an uncaring womaniser than to admit what I was really beginning to feel. Oh, Max, I'm so sorry.''

"No need to apologise." He grinned mockingly down at her. "You can spend the rest of your life making amends to me, instead.''

"You'd better believe it." She laughed back at him, all restraint gone, all inhibitions fled.

"Oh, I do," he said. "And it can't begin too soon." He bent his head, biting delicately at the lobe of her ear. He murmured, "They say that the climax to making love is like dying a little death, and I'm going to make you die a thousand deaths for every harsh word, every bad moment you've made me suffer.''

Ginny pulled away from him a little, making a face of mock-alarm, "Is that a threat?''

"No," said Max, and smiled down at her. "A promise, my darling.''

He kissed her again, and as she surrendered eagerly to the urgent hunger of his lips, Ginny knew that their future together promised all the happiness she would ever need.

Harlequin Presents...

The books that let you escape
into the wonderful world of romance!
Trips to exotic places...interesting
plots...meeting memorable people...
the excitement of love....These are
integral parts of Harlequin Presents—
the heartwarming novels read by
women everywhere.

Many early issues are now available.
Choose from this great selection!